A WEE]

Bett Rose

Printed by PublishingPush Ltd

Dedication

This book is dedicated to my readers,

For those who have a little time and want to read a simple story, with the focus on human nature and relationships.

For those who have time on their hands after a working lifetime.

For those who dream of writing stories and novels and who have not yet made a start.

For those of you who have self-doubt or low esteem.

I offer you all my gentle encouragement, just as my Guide encouraged me,

"Just do it, Betty, Sit down and write."

Contents

Introduction

WW2 was known as the Second World War. It was a global war that lasted from 1st September 1939 - 2nd September 1945.

In 1938 the Nazis invaded Austria and then Czechoslovakia.
On 1st September 1939 Nazi troups invaded Poland.

The UK and France gave Hitler an Ultimatum. They threatened war if his troops were not withdrawn by 3rd September 1939.

Hitler ignored the threat.

France and UK declared war.

There were two major alliances.

Axis powers Germany, Italy and Japan.

Allies, France, China, UK, Canada, Australia and New Zealand.

The United States joint the allies on December 11 1941, 4 days after Japan attacked Pearl Harbour.

The Soviet Union joined the allies in June 1941 after Germany attacked it.

Spain, Sweden, Switzerland and Ireland stayed neutral.

Families in the UK heard the news on the radio announced by the Prime Minister, Neville Chamberlain at 11.15am.

"This country is at war with Germany."

This is a story of everyday lives and relationships, of working-class neighbours and families living out their reality of WW2 Britain.

Just a short story - that includes laughter and light and hope and disappointments and compassion, and most importantly, a happy ending.

CHAPTER 1.

Frances gazed down into her blue china teacup. Turning the cup to the left and right, she stared hard. She found the warmth from the cup strangely comforting.

Frances felt empty inside; her husband Joseph had been reported missing following the defence and desperate evacuation of the British and Allied forces from the French seaport of Dunkirk, in May/June 1940. Naval ships and hundreds of all types of fishing and civilian boats from England had travelled across the channel with Air cover provided by fighter aircraft and despite very heavy losses from German attack and the Luftwaffe bombs thousands of British, French and Belgium troops were rescued and brought home.

But not Joseph!

It was commonly thought that Hitler had expected Britain to try and negotiate some sort of peace at this time, after all, the war was not going well for Britain as Germany had already invaded Denmark and Norway, Luxemburg, Netherlands, and Belgium had made inroads into France.

Joseph's war had been short, lasting only a matter of months following his 'call up' in September 1939 when Britain and France had declared war on Nazi Germany following the Nazi invasion of Poland.

The Soviet Union had joined the Allies in

June, 1941, after Germany had turned its attention to her and attacked them. Shortly following this Japan attacked Pearl Harbour's American Naval Base and so the United States of America also joined the Allies in December, 1941.

It was now nearly three years since Frances had received her telegram, she was just 29 years old, and classed as a widow. Her marriage to Joseph had not produced any children despite their closeness and her longing for a family.

At this moment she was tired and lonely. In her darkest moments, she acknowledged that maybe she should accept her friend's advice that she was a widow and that she should move on. But for some reason that she could not explain she could not let go of the hope that he had somehow, somewhere, survived. Frances was aware of the glances and whispers of concern amongst her friends and understood the rationale that it was an unlikely probability that Joseph had survived after all of this time, but she stubbornly clung on to her belief that if her husband had passed then she would know, deep inside, that her soul mate had gone.

Frances existed, for now, working 12-hour shifts in the engineering factory, standing at a Press machine, doing a Man's work for half of the pay. Her work was designated as semi-skilled and therefore classed as 'Women's Work and deserving of Women's rates of pay. Most days Frances would slide out of bed at 5 am to start her 12-hour shift and trudge home in the blackout around 6 pm in the evening. For the last two months, she had been working overtime, even more than the regulation 55 hours that were advised as a maximum to maintain the worker's safety. Today she had volunteered to work a Sunday and halfway through the shift she had started to regret her decision, but she had pushed on and exhausted, made her way home in the dark, to an empty house, again.

Midnight would sometimes be waiting on the front doorstep and he would brush his furry body against her ankles and meow a loud welcome. Joseph had loved his sleek handsome cat dearly and Midnight had never really settled since his master had failed to come home. Frances was so pleased on the occasions when Midnight was waiting for her, tonight especially. He was certainly a beauty with his glossy black shining fur coat and four snow white paws. He remained plump despite the wartime rationing of food. Midnight found that the bombed-out sites provided a rich source of food available which sustained his appetite and satisfied his innate hunting instincts. Tonight as Frances sat in her chair he was content to curl up on her feet and his mistress was very glad of his warmth and his company.

Frances rented a room out to Eliza who was 27 years old and married to Thomas, a Merchant Seaman. Eliza had 3-year-old twin boys Charley and Michael who were staying with their Gran and Granddad on their farm at the edge of the small town.

Eliza also worked at the same engineering factory as Frances but they worked opposite shifts mostly so they could go days without catching up with each other for a good gossip or a meal. Sometimes the two women were placed on shift together but there still wasn't much opportunity to talk because the working environment was noisy with the sound of hammers and drills and other heavy machinery working. Although they were both reasonably young women they found that having to stand for long hours at their machines was exhausting and sometimes, 'if they were pushed' for an order, they would only have a 10-minute break before starting again. This didn't happen too often because the trade unions frowned on such practice, tiredness caused accidents. Sometimes Eliza would watch other women who were in their forties and fifties wearily 'clock on' for the 12-hour shift and she would wonder, 'Goodness knows how the older ladies managed but they did.'

Eliza knew that it was not compulsory for her to register for work because she had children under the age of 14 years but she needed to help out with the twins keep and beside this her husband's pay in the Merchant Navy was poor. Eliza and the other women knew that their effort in wartime production was vital and Eliza took a pride in contributing along with the others. She was aware that the twins were safer staying with her parents on the farm and the truth was that she also relished the independence that her wages and staying with Frances gave her.

As a young girl and the only child growing up on the farm, her father had been very strict and protective of his only daughter and she certainly did not want to repeat that experience again. Eliza knew that her father would "see it as my duty" to keep her safe whilst Thomas was away and although she understood that he meant well she was determined that she would not be going back home.

When the opportunity arose then Eliza would visit the twins and enjoy every moment but on these visits, she could see that they were healthy and happy and had a freedom that they could only have on the farm. Eliza would finish the visit content that all was for the best and she would return with provisions of jam and a couple fresh eggs which were relished by herself and Frances as a wonderful replacement for the dreadful dried eggs that they usually had to make do with. On her return, Eliza would wait up for Frances and they would share a dish of scrambled eggs and have a long chat before the routine began again. The two women had become good friends and although they were very different in personality they 'rubbed along famously' as Eliza liked to say to reassure her dad.

Now Frances was known as the beauty in the street. She was tall and willowy and she turned heads when she walked by with a delicate grace that would have inspired a thousand artists to beg to paint her portrait. Her long coal black hair that flowed down her back would fall over her face and hide a shy smile and a glance from her emerald green eyes framed by thick ebony lashes would cause many males to become hot under his collar. It could be said that Frances did not need to be short of males' attention. However, Frances was not interested, not in the slightest!

Frances made no attempt to attract attention and she had very little interest in receiving compliments, in fact, she found this made her feel very uncomfortable. The anonymity of wearing overalls and a turban for her daily duties suited her well. The deep red lipstick that Joseph had loved her to wear never came out of its case. Frances still carried an aching in her heart and her being for her man. She found that her nights were often still disturbed by dreams that he was calling out her name and then he would be holding her in his arms tenderly as he used to. She found that work anesthetised the pain to some extent but the nights could still be long and her bed cold.

Her lodger, Eliza loved flattery and male attention. They were 'as different as chalk and cheese' in this respect. Eliza thrilled for the sweet talk and the male recognition of her womanly charms! Eliza was a flirt that's true and she could see no harm in this. She enjoyed wearing her strawberry blonde hair in the latest styles and would often copy the 1940s film stars hairstyles and makeup. Eliza's favourite was a classic up-do of straight up the back with lots of curls on top or maybe a side parting and soft waves. At work she was obliged to wear her hair up but she hid her pin curls under her scarf for later. Wearing Powder and lipstick were second nature to her but sometimes the turban did come in handy when the shortage of shampoo or water rationing meant that her hair was not as perfectly coloured as she would like it to be.

The wearing of turbans to keep hair out of the way of heavy machinery was mandatory and also practical during these times. Because of cosmetics being in short supply Eliza would sometimes resort to using beetroot as a stain for her lips and cheeks, for Eliza deemed it unthinkable that she would not make the best of herself. Although cosmetic houses still advertised they were not always able to meet demand during these times of shortages but Government posters encouraged women to continue looking presentable and feminine and to make an effort as a means of boosting morale. Eliza needed no encouragement. Petit and shapely Eliza had corn blue eyes framed with honey blonde lashes and she fluttered these lashes knowingly to gain a full advantage.

Thomas was away on his ship supplying and escorting. Eliza missed male company and enjoyed compliments, "Why ever not? It's what makes the world go around" she would laugh. Eliza never knew when Thomas's ship would make it to shore, she didn't allow herself to think of his ship going down, and that was too unbearable a prospect!

Next door lived Mrs Pickering and her husband Arthur. Their two sons, James and Gordon were away from home serving in the RAF. Arthur was out of the house for a lot of the time serving as a fire warden and the raids were keeping him busy most nights. Joanie didn't complain, but she secretly had concerns about her husband being able to keep this level of activity up for much longer. Arthur was not a young man and his health was compromised by the frequent chest infections that ravaged his body during each spell of cold damp weather.

Arthur was a proud man; very much a gentleman and he believed strongly that whilst the young men were away fighting, those left behind needed to pull together too. Arthur had been a grammar schoolmaster for all of his working life until the age of 63 years when he had to retire early because of an increased frailty which did not stand him in a good place to manage classes of rowdy boys. However, the shortage of teachers during the war meant that some of the schools were closed and many of the children were receiving a very 'patchy' education, if any at all. Arthur took classes two days a week at the church hall teaching 'the three R's, reading, writing and arithmetic for he strongly believed that these working-class children should not be neglected in their need for literacy and basic adding up and 'times tables.'

When not engaged in his Fire Warden Duties and teaching he would spend time on the communal allotment a street away. Once he was there he would happily potter and dig and engage with the few poultry that strutted and pecked at the earth for the worms and feed that he would scatter amongst them. Joanie joined him when she could and he was always pleased to see his plump little wife pedalling along towards him wearing her flowered apron, her hair pulled back in a bun and wearing a large smile. Joanie's face would be red with the exertion of riding the bicycle and she would clatter into the shed with relief, laughing and giggling like the young girl that she used to be when they first met. They would spend an hour together quietly engaged in weeding or gathering or just sitting and pondering about the future or talking of the daily trivialities of wartime life. Somehow they both skirted the topic of their boys being away fighting. They were both more than aware of the danger that their sons faced each time they flew with their squadron but they found verbalising their fears didn't help either of them cope with this reality.

Arthur had ensured that both of their sons had received a good standard of education and Gordon had been all set to go to University to study the sciences whilst Gordon had chosen a career in engineering. The outbreak of war in the 3rd year of their chosen work/life path had seen them sign up for the RAF and Joanie had been 'besides herself' with frustration and worry. Joanie had been in her late thirties when she had her sons, a year apart, and following their difficult births Arthur had been advised that his wife should not go through childbirth again. Arthur had taken the Doctor's advice seriously and he and Joanie had taken to having separate beds. Arthur was 14 years older than his wife and he had heard many men laughing off such advice from their doctors only to regret it at a later date when their wife had died from complications whilst going into labour at home. He had been clear that this wasn't about to happen to his wife, "Not for all the tea in China.." Joanie had been very relieved that Arthur had reacted to the doctor's news in a respectful way. She was very aware of the risk of further childbirth having lost a good friend in childbirth who had not had such an understanding husband. Joanie had been content with her two boys and her genteel husband and she was very aware that she had made the right choice when she had accepted Arthur's offer of marriage rather than her earlier beau who had been very attractive and nearer her own age. Joanie's friends had 'taken the Mick' but time had proved her right.

Joanie muddled on, passing much of her time queuing for rations and doing odd jobs for the women in the street that were working in the factories around about. Sometimes she helped out with the children that had not been evacuated and remained at home or she would give Arthur 'a hand' down at the church Hall with his classes.

When she received a letter from the boys she would race down to the allotment and she and Arthur would read the news together, usually two or three times before she was ready to put it away in her apron pocket. The letters were stored away in her sewing box and she would always take the box to the shelter when there was a raid, not wanting to lose them if the house took a hit.

Mrs Norma Watling and her four girls lived in the house on the other side of Frances. Her four girls were aged between 8 years and 13 years and the family was noisy and generally happy and well. The girls loved to help out on the allotment when they were not at school or "run a few errands for a few treats" for the older residents in the street. Sweets were few and far between, sugar was scarce and sometimes Norma preferred to swap the sweet rations for something more substantial when she could. Besides, the girls weren't keen on the hot liquorice Imps and Fishermans Friends that were usually all that was for sale in the shops at the present.

The girls' father Reginald was away overseas with the Engineering Corps, he had narrowly missed the first draft to war service because he was just over the 41-years-age limit but he had qualified when the age limit had been raised to 51 years of age. Reg had been ready to 'do his bit' and he had laughingly reassured a worried Norma that "there's a lot of life left in me yet, you should know that." Norma had blushed and scolded him for 'talking smutty' in front of the girls but she was more than aware that the war was not going in their favour and that the British army needed every available, healthy man.

Norma was frightened for Reg when he had been 'called up,' after all, 'he wasn't a young man' but she had reminded herself of the words of their great leader, Winston Churchill, who had replaced the Prime Minister Neville Chamberlain and in her mind was 'The man for the job.' He had been right when he had gravely warned them that this would not be an easy fight but he had reassured his people that he believed if they all pulled together then they had a chance, and this gave her hope. Reginald Watling had waved goodbye to his wife and family, keen at last to be in uniform and joining in the action.

The girls were devastated. They missed his teasing, the way he used to come home from the pub at Sunday lunchtime and twirl a protesting Norma around whilst she was trying to dish up the Sunday dinner in the kitchen. They missed the way he used to towel dry their hair after their Saturday afternoon bath. They missed the smell of his cigarettes and his plonking on the piano when they had a get-together. All four girls missed the feeling of safety when their father was around, the older 13-year Mary particularly. Norma was jolly and generous and kept the girls busy with knitting and baking and jigsaws but when the planes came over they wanted Dad.

Sometimes Norma cooked for Frances and Eliza using her precious aluminium saucepans which had escaped the collections for scrap metal. She knew that the metal was used towards making Spitfires and other essential equipment but Norma decided that the two that she had kept were needed and that she had given up quite enough. After all, the playgrounds were empty, the children's slides and swings had been dismantled and taken away for the steel which was used towards making tanks and guns and surely a couple of saucepans could be excused, couldn't they? She justified her conscience with the knowledge that she provided meals for the girls when they were working such long shifts, whilst she protested 'They can't beat Adolf on empty bellies can they?'

She liked to keep her girls close at home but she knew they had to have some fresh air, 'if you could call it that.' For most days the air was full of dust and ashes and the streets were littered with glass and sometimes worse! Her girls had to settle mostly for a skipping rope in the backyard or a game of 'two ball' on the entry wall instead.

Norma enjoyed cooking and baking and because her stove was heated with wood or coal, she wasn't inconvenienced too much if there was damage to the gas pipes or electricity following a raid or fires. It heated the kitchen up nicely and provided a cosy haven for the girls, and 'that cat from over the road that seemed to like making his home in front of it lately.'

For most of her days, Norma would find herself standing in line in the cold, queuing for food rations. In the Summer and early autumn, she had taken the girls blackberry picking and collecting windfall apples, pears, and hazelnuts from the country lanes and derelict gardens. This was a wonderful bounty because she never knew when fresh produce would be in the shops. In the summer she would keep the little meat that she was allowed to buy in a small cupboard to keep the flies off and she would grandly call this her meat safe. The girls would laugh, "You're meant to keep money in a safe mum" and she would insist that the meat was worth more than gold coins in these days.

Norma loved the smell of freshly baked bread and cakes and one of the wartime favourites that she involved the girls in making was bread pudding. Any stale bread was soaked in milk or cold tea if she couldn't get the milk and then mixed with some sort of spread and spices with dried raisins or any dried mixed fruit that she could get her hands on. Fresh eggs were rationed and so she would add a little-dried egg to the mixture, spice was also a luxury but the women in the street often pooled their resources. It made a lovely stodgy sweet pudding, even sweeter if she had real sugar and not the saccharine substitute that always left a bitter aftertaste in your mouth. They all missed having butter on their bread too, the margarine that was meant to be a substitute was really only fit for baking, but they were assured that it was good for their health and the fact that it contained vitamin D that helped to prevent the girls developing rickets meant that she would scrape it onto their toast, much to their disgust. Still, her baking filled the girl's bellies and satisfied their craving for something sweet and it kept Norma from having too much time on her hands for brooding. Frances and Eliza loved it too and Lizzie, the elderly lady that Ruby lodged with, would sometimes send over her own tasty speciality, a basin of brawn which she made from boiling a sheep's head in the hope of a swap.

Folks around the streets were mostly decent and honest and with the shortage of food, they had become accustomed to sharing and helping each other out. Swedes, carrots, and parsnips were fairly plentiful as the Government gave out seeds to those who had big allotments and the women had become quite inventive with their recipes. Norma's speciality was carrot scones and potato shortbread and she'd even tried making rhubarb jam using dates to substitute the shortage of sugar.

Harold and Violet lived in a tiny two-up two-down detached cottage next to the allotment. Harold was in his mid-seventies and Violet was slightly younger in her late sixties but Harold was the more spritely of the two and he spent a lot of his time at the allotment or playing darts at the pub when he had funds. Harold had an old horse and cart and he would drive slowly around the streets collecting scraps for a pig that he kept up on the allotment. Rufus was getting on in years but Harold would drive him slowly, chatting to him and rubbing his greying black neck and mane as they trundled along. The horse had belonged to his boys Eric and Clive and they had passed many a good time with him when they were in their teens.

The boys also owned a Black Labrador called 'Scoffer' for the simple reason of his ability to pinch any bit of spare food going if you carelessly took your eyes off it. In this respect of his training, and they had had him from a young pup just weaned from his mother, they had been unsuccessful. Other than that Scoffer was a good and faithful pet and guard dog and Violet liked to keep him at home with her when Harold was out of the house. He reminded her of her boys and the house didn't feel so lonely when he was around. Scoffer was getting on in years now, her sons had been in their late teens when they had brought him back with them one Christmas and

Harold had insisted that the pup would be their responsibility to keep and to train and they had keenly agreed, succeeding in all aspects other than his refusal to respect the boundaries of ownership of food.

Today Harold wasn't best pleased that bread had been used to make a pudding. The pig was communal responsibility and they were all meant to take a part in providing food before they would all eventually share in the meat. Norma managed to placate Harold by wrapping up two slices of the warm bread pudding in greaseproof paper and popping it into his overall pocket. Harold relented and smiled.

Eric and Clive were also away fighting with The First British Army which also included French and American units. Harold was aware that the boys were overseas but he was unaware of any more details. Both sons had been called up within two weeks of each other and had looked at this event with excitement and were eager for what they believed was to be an adventure. Harold believed that the boys were in for a bit of a hard lesson but hid his reservations. He could see no point in distressing Violet who believed that "the war would never last as long as the last one."

Neither of the boys was married or courting despite being in their late twenties and both had notions of meeting foreign exotic girls. Harold was keen to warn them both of the importance of keeping a moral stance, he was well aware of the Venereal diseases that were often prolific within the Armed Forces and his sons were healthy lads who had never really strayed far from home. Harold had taken them both aside on this point and spoke to them out of the hearing range of their Mother! "We are just popping down the local Vi, be back after a swift half."

Violet sighed to herself, she'd heard that a few times before! Violet knew that the boys had to do their bit and she was proud of them both looking very smart in their Khaki. She was troubled though, troubled by a fear that even if they survived the fighting then she would still never see them again. She couldn't shake this mood off no matter how much she tried and she was thinking of popping around to ask her friend Lizzie if she could show some light on this with her cards.

Violet had carried two girl babies but lost them both in her later stages of pregnancy and so she had been in her thirties when she and Harold had tried again and successfully had the two boys close together. Harold had been as proud as punch with his sons and worked hard to provide for them all. He'd played hard as well, stopping off at the pub most evenings after work for a pint and a game of darts or cards before calling in at the allotment and then finally home, about 9 pm. Harold didn't keep Violet short but she never knew how much he brought home in his wage packet each week either. Eric and Clive had followed in their father's footsteps working in Carpentry, first as apprentices and then having their papers after five years. They had both brought money into the house and Violet had never had to go out to work or take a little cleaning job to make ends meet as did some of her friends. She knew that she was lucky that way.

Weekends Harold would spend on the allotment with the boys, growing vegetables and fruit trees and showing them how to take care of Rufus who he'd won in a game of cards one Christmas. Harold had never been unfaithful as far as Violet was aware, but she knew that he had an eye for a beautiful woman, and the boys were the same. She had long given up the hope of grandchildren and she would have loved to have had a daughter in law, especially after losing her two girls. Yes, she would pay a visit to Lizzie when she had the chance! She might even have a catch up with Lizzie's lodger Ruby. Ruby was always full of life and it would be a tonic to have a cup of tea and a chin wag with them both.

Ruby stayed with Lizzie and she was Frances's very best friend. Frances often thought that she wouldn't have got through the past year without Ruby.

Ruby loved the Yanks, The Yanks loved Ruby. They loved her womanly curves, her flaming, auburn shoulder length hair, and her warm brown friendly eyes which were framed with pencilled brows drawn in a high arch. "What a doll" was the usual comment when Ruby passed through the base. Ruby perfumed and polished her legs with a pumice stone. Ruby had silk stockings. Ruby had a wonderfully deep soulful singing voice and she loved to entertain with her favourite songs made popular by Billie Holiday and Doris Day. Ruby would bring Lizzie to tears when she sang any song of Vera Lyn's.

Ruby enjoyed living near the USAAF base and she managed to find employment there. The American Air Force base was a major servicing facility for fighters and heavy bombers providing support for the many Air Force divisions. Many thousands of service men and women lived on the huge base with some living in the surrounding area. The US Army and Air Force had arrived later on in the war and the locals found themselves to be outnumbered in some areas. For many, the initial annoyance and suspicion lessened as time went on and the need for American support was appreciated and welcomed. Sometimes fighting broke out but for the most part, the Americans were eventually accepted and in fact some thought that they brought a touch of glamour into their lives.

Visits with the Americans also brought white creamy soap wrapped in tissue paper which was so heavenly to use compared to the huge blocks of dark green disinfectant smelling soap that was all they could buy with their coupons. The local townsfolk tried peanuts and chewing gum for the first time and the divine creamy chocolate bars, and for girls like Ruby, there were silk stockings and perfume and decent cigarettes instead of the strange Turkish brands that were usually the only ones available.

Some families invited the American soldiers into their homes for tea and their company reminded them of their own sons away fighting. Many friendships were formed, and some developed into relationships which were frowned on by a few. The dances and American music with the Big band sounds and jitterbugging were new and exciting and very much enjoyed on both sides. Ruby and Eliza were amongst those, they welcomed any activity that would break the stagnant routine of their lives.

Ruby and Frances had grown up together, they had attended the same schools until they both reached 14 years and were placed into service as housemaids. Frances had met her Joseph who had worked as a gardener with the same family. Frances had married Joseph in her late teens and he had made her happy, she had never had eyes for anyone else.

Ruby was bright and energetic and the role of housemaid did not suit her personality or her abilities. Ruby had been very bright at school, excelling in mathematics and able to speak French fluently, learnt from her French grandmother. Ruby was expected to bring a wage into the house and her father believed that a higher education for his daughter would be wasted as he expected his daughter to be married before long like many young girls did. Ruby played ball for a while but as soon as she was able she found work as a barmaid and waitress in a local hotel and where she was given a room as part of her wages.

The work was not glamorous but she had her independence and time off each day and she enjoyed the lively chatter over the bar. Ruby's father was angry and refused to have her home after this. Ruby coped!

The friendship between Ruby and Frances continued and when Joseph and Frances left service to start up a small business sometimes Frances invited Ruby to stay with her and Joseph for a weekend. Frances felt that this would make up for some of the family time that Ruby had missed out on. Ruby enjoyed the home cooking and the laughter and stories shared between them of some of the antics of the customers at the hotel and of their past life in service, but Ruby didn't miss her parents. Her grandmother had passed away and her parents had not made a happy home; if this was marriage she would not be chasing after a groom that was for sure.

Frances and Joseph? Well maybe their marriage was the exception.

Joseph had set up a hardware shop and a small garden centre with his severance pay when his employers had decided to sell up and move to London. They had been very fond of Joseph and had treated the couple very well and with Frances's savings they were well set up. The business was thriving and Joseph was able to put a deposit down on a nice little-terraced house and then let out the flat above the shop. Then war broke out and Frances had waved Joseph goodbye wearing her red lipstick and a smile until the train disappeared and then she had turned and wept. Joseph's aunt and uncle took over the business and the flat and she moved into the house that Joseph had bought for them.

Frances and Ruby both registered for work and had been interviewed and placed in essential wartime occupations. Frances had been placed in engineering and Ruby had been sent off for training at some establishment for two months before returning to work at the base. Ruby moved in with Lizzie because Frances had taken Eliza in as a lodger during this time. Ruby now rode off to the local USAAF base on her bicycle early each morning and came home each evening, never discussing her work. Frances eventually fell into a routine at the factory, taking one day at a time and not really thinking too far forward in the beginning year. Gradually she began to get friendly with her neighbours; one in particular was Lizzie, the widowed lady who Ruby shared with. Frances's interest in looking into the future and reading tea leaves began with Lizzie.

Lizzie with the penetrating black-brown eyes that seemed to look right into your soul. Lizzie with the aged and wizened face and the kindest smile that you would ever see. Lizzie found a way to offer comfort to them all in their times of need. She would welcome them with a smile and her intense gaze and ask them in at the drop of a hat. She offered comfort and mystery and a refuge. Lizzie was everybody's friend and she had been pleased to rent out a room to Ruby.

Ruby had instantly liked the elderly lady who had offered her a home, she was small and dark and welcoming and she had reminded her of her French grandmother. Ruby was aware of Lizzie's reputation as a person who could see into the future and talk to those who had passed and as far as she was concerned there was a need for these sorts of womanly skills, which she believed could give great comfort in times of distress and loss. The two women 'got along famously' and Ruby found the notion of living with the local wise woman exciting.

Many of the streets around echoed the pattern of women living alone or sharing with other women whilst their menfolk were away fighting. The men who were too old to fight or those men who worked in reserved occupations or who were exempt from service on medical grounds still took an active part in essential services such as Fire Wardens, drivers, plumbers or farm workers.

Although most of the children were evacuated for their safety, many were still kept at home for various reasons and schools did their best to provide an education. This was sometimes patchy and very

23

basic because teachers had also been drafted and so retired teachers were sometimes brought in to 'hold the fort.'

Norma's girls who were now back home after an unsuccessful evacuation took full advantage of these circumstances and knew that if they feigned an upset tummy then there were very few repercussions.

Norma had taken up the Government's offer of evacuation for her girls although their town wasn't classified in the evacuation zone initially. It had almost 'broken' her heart when she had seen them off at the train station. They had looked completely bewildered as they stood in line with the other children, carrying their little cardboard suitcases from Woolworths and their gas mask cases and the youngest still holding tightly onto her teddy. She hadn't been given any information about where their destination was to be other than to be advised that she would receive a postcard from the girls when they were billeted and settled. She had eagerly waited for their postcard and been surprised and pleased to read that they were all found a home together.

Her relief hadn't lasted for long. Norma had collected 'her chicks' following an impulsive visit which had resulted in angry words and their swift return home. She was aware of the risk but she would 'face the music' with Reg and she had written explaining immediately.

Norma took care that her girls didn't join the gangs of the children who were to be found playing on the 'Bombsites' and the many waste grounds that held the sad remains of homes and places of work that the Luftwaffe had destroyed. She didn't want them bringing home trophies of shrapnel either, she found it distressing and didn't want them in her home. She did her best to keep them busy, they were good girls and at the moment they were particularly clingy after their evacuation experience.

"Evacuation Pied Piper, my arse," Norma had retorted on seeing the conditions that she found her girls in when she had visited. They had followed her out of the door like a row of eager ducklings, the older daughter giggling at 'mum's rude words.'.'

The eldest could often be found at Lizzie's house playing draughts or having a cup of sweet tea with a biscuit. There was something about Lizzie's house that appealed to Mary. It felt safe like her own home used to before their dad Reg had gone away.

Back at Lizzie's when the sirens screamed out she would take herself under the stairs. If Ruby was at home then they would go down into their Anderson shelter in the back garden and they would huddle together to keep themselves warm until the 'all clear' sounded. Sometimes they would be 'holed up' there for hours and despite thick blankets and extra coats, the damp seeped into Lizzie's old bones. If Ruby was working then Lizzie would clamber under the stairs, shut the cupboard door and say her prayers. So far they had been answered.

Women in the surrounding streets called on Lizzie when they were at their wits end, when they had a strange dream, when they didn't have two halfpennies to rub together or when they needed some excitement in the drab, routine, grey, dismal war days. Sometimes they would be alone, sometimes in threes or fours they would knock on her door and ask Lizzie to 'look into my cup' and tell them of their future. Lizzie knew most of them well and she believed in giving comfort when she could. In Lizzie's experience the tea leaves gave encouragement and caution, but sometimes she kept a forewarning to herself and managed to give a version of the signs in the cup that would not generate fear or alarm. Wasn't each day hard enough? Money didn't change hands but she wasn't too proud to refuse a bit of whatever groceries were offered on occasion. She believed in the exchange of energy for luck. Hence she often had a bit of sugar or a biscuit for one of Norma's girls.

Frances would join in these sessions whenever she could and she would watch intently while Lizzie practiced her art and the more she saw the more she wanted to try. For Lizzie's skill was an art, handed down to her through the generations along with a responsibility to ensure that her readings would not be harmful and that they always gave comfort. Frances was fascinated when Lizzie read the Tarot cards and gazed at misty shapes in the depths of the crystal seeing ball. She decided that reading the tea leaves was a step far enough for her because she somehow feared the shadows in the crystal ball and the Tarot cards with their deck of 78 powerful symbols. Frances found the tea leaf readings a comfort and had a whim to try and develop the skill. Lizzie knew Frances well enough to know that she was a sensitive person and she was willing to work with her and let her try. Frances did not claim to own any psychic ability but Lizzie was aware that in Frances's case this could be developed.

CHAPTER 2.

So, Frances stared intently into her teacup. She turned it to the left and the right. She looked down into the bottom, at the side for not too distant events and at the rim for the present. She made a wish, asking that the tea leaves would show her true events and her destiny. Frances saw lines and dots but no significant shapes or symbols that she could identify. She saw nothing that gave her hope, nothing that would lift her heart or her energy. All she could make out were dots travelling from the base of the cup to the rim. She thought back to some of Lizzie's teachings and concentrated. What did they mean? A journey maybe? Who's journey then? Mine? She pondered! As much as she wished she didn't see any birds or hearts, not this time.

Placing the cup and saucer down beside her she closed her eyes. Midnight purred and snuggled in closer moving onto her lap. Frances sighed, "I'll just have forty winks, I'm so weary and my feet are absolutely throbbing after standing at that machine all day puss." Frances's head fell forward and Midnight hopped down and padded over to the corner of the darkened room, staring at the skirting board with keen interest.

Glenn Miller and his band were playing Moonlight Serenade and Frances and Joseph were moving around the hall amongst the jostling of other couples. Frances felt that she was floating in his arms as the band with their clarinets and trumpets played their smooth sophisticated melodies. Joseph gazed down into her face and their eyes locked and their lips were almost touching. The band changed the tune to a slow seductive Beguine by Arty Shaw and Joseph coiled a lock of her long black silky hair around his fingers and they danced and swayed together. Joseph hummed softly and kissed the back of her neck and buried his face into her hair.

The music changed again to Sentimental Journey and Frances whispered "Let's go Home."

The energy between them was vibrant and when Joseph brushed his hand down the smoothness of her dress as it clung to her thigh Frances caught her breath. Joseph squeezed her hand and they pushed their way through the many couples as the music changed to a lively 'Minnie's in the Money' by Benny Goodman. The dancers were pulling and pushing and twirling in the jive and as the Swing got into action nimble feet danced to the rhythm and the pounding of the piano. Petticoats and skirts twirled and females were flung over their partners' shoulder and through their uniformed legs. Faces were red, the band was loud and for now the crowds were able to forget everything but the excitement and love and laughter that filled the dance room.

This was the last night of Joseph's leave and normally the pair would be stamping and jumping along with the rest to the latest music and the dances introduced by the American G I's. But tonight it was different. Joseph's eyes were on his wife and his brown eyes smouldered. Pushing their way through they were soon out of the heat and the noise and they clung onto each other tightly, laughing. Suddenly stinging icy cold rain slammed against Frances's face and the cold harsh wind made her catch her breath.

"Frances wake up."

She woke to the scream of the sirens. The top window was slightly ajar and cold raindrops were pouring through the gap and running down her face. The room was in darkness from the blackness inside and the blackness outside. There was a new moon and very little light.

Frances was shivering. Who called her? She and Midnight were alone. As the sirens screamed out their warning she grabbed for the crouching cat but he dashed away into the hall and up the stairs.

Disorientated Frances felt her way along the cold damp walls and through to the scullery. She clambered down the three stone steps at the back door and entered the safety of the Anderson shelter. Once again she was alone and cold and she wondered how Eliza was getting on whilst working the night shift. Frances wrapped the blankets around her tightly and she leant against the corrugated walls and closed her eyes. She tried to recapture the interrupted dream but sleep escaped her. Hugging herself she managed to doze lightly, the memory of her and Joseph dancing together was still vivid and although painful it was somehow a comfort.

Time passed and Frances stopped trying to go back to sleep, knowing that the factories around had ceased sounding the works hooter when war broke out so that it would not be confused with the warning sirens meant that Frances was wary of falling into a deep sleep now and missing her shift. Being on shift at 6 am meant that she needed to be up and washed and ready to make the 30-minute walk to work for

5.30 am. The air raids had virtually destroyed the bus services and most now used 'Shanks Pony' or a bicycle if they were lucky enough to own one. Frances had given her bike to Ruby and so she would join the many others on the street walking into work. Frances sat in the blackness whilst the night vibrated with shouts and gunfire and thuds and she hugged herself and cried silent tears for Joe. Frances prayed that she wouldn't be the victim of a straight hit. Maybe she was lonely but she wasn't ready to die in this way.

"Not by a German Bomb anyway," she whispered.

Her neighbour Lizzie sat underneath the stairs amongst the mops and brushes and she was becoming impatient. It was becoming hot and stuffy and she was feeling irritable. Besides everything else she 'needed a pee' and she had forgotten to take her 'Gus under' into the cupboard with her.

"If I've got to go I'll go in my own place, in my own home" she muttered to herself as she shifted around trying to get more comfortable.

If Ruby had returned from the base then she would have made the effort to join her in the shelter but as often as not Ruby would stay over if the weather was particularly bad or if the bombing had started before she left for home. Lizzie didn't ask too many questions, she knew Ruby was sharp and independent and that she would be taken care of if she stayed at the base.

"Ah, in one way or another" she smiled.

Ruby, head down had just started to cycle

home when the night sky had lit up and the sirens called out their warning. She had made this solitary journey home many times before through these dark country lanes. Visibility was particularly poor tonight because of the new moon but she often joked that she could travel this way home blindfolded because she had cycled the journey so many times. White lines had been painted down the middle of the road and on the curbs to aid visibility which was some help and she sometimes used her small torch that she'd been issued with, that is if she could get hold of some batteries. It didn't give a lot of light out but she kept it in her pocket anyway feeling safer with the knowledge that she had it.

Tonight the rain was lashing down in sheets and Ruby shivered, it seemed that the blackness that surrounded her was touching her. Overhead came the thundering of aircraft and flashes of light shot across the blackness of the night sky. Ruby had little choice but to cycle forward into the rain or perhaps to try and shelter underneath a tree. As she pushed forward she could feel the fear and adrenaline coursing through her body and her heart pounded and lurched in her chest at each thud or whistle or scream.

Ruby was just a dark shadow hurtling along, well hidden in her heavy grey coat and trousers and black headscarf which hid her heavy auburn curls. She rarely wore her luminous arm bans because there were very few car users on these lanes other than jeeps from the base. Petrol was strictly rationed anyway and speed was restricted to 20mph during the blackout so she wasn't anticipating meeting any vehicles at this time of night. She would hear the engine sound of a jeep easily before she met it. Ruby smiled to herself remembering the many posters encouraging people to eat plenty of carrots to aid vision in the darkness. "One thing there isn't a shortage of, blinking carrots."

Next minute she heard a screeching of tyres and a male voice shouting "Hells bells" and Ruby toppled off her bike, falling sideways into the hedge. She struggled to push the bike's weight off her whilst trying to get some sort of balance. The branches were sharp and she tried to brush the wet leaves from her hair as she tried to stand but she was hampered by the heaviness of her wet coat. Ruby struggled and as she wiped the wetness from her stinging cheeks a torch shone into her face. She found herself being pulled up roughly onto her feet.

"I'd know that perfume anywhere Ruby, are you okay sugar?" a deep male voice enquired.

"I'm a bit shaky and soaking wet and I'm not sure about my bike."

Her voice trembled and she clearly sounded distressed. Trying to disengage the bicycle from the hedge she stumbled.

"Ouch, I'm scratched to heck and I've lost my blinking headscarf" she cried and she tried to wipe away tears of frustration.

The male voice offered help and she recognised the slow American drawl, "Here babe, sit in the jeep, it was lucky that I was only driving in grandma gear. Why didn't you stay at the base?"

"Wish I had now" she blustered, embarrassed and very conscious of looking 'a sight.'

"I'll put your bike on the back and I best get you back with me, we can't do anything else while this raid goes on."

Ruby didn't argue and she recognised the officer from the American base where she worked. He was always friendly and informal despite his rank and he had never once 'overstepped the mark' with her during her time there. She climbed in beside him, thankful and suddenly feeling weary and very cold in her wet clothes. The jeep sped forward and Ruby clung on as they bumped over the many dips and holes in the country lanes.

Lieutenant Parker was aware of Ruby's work and the effect that she had on the men. He liked to keep his ear to the ground and although protocol ensured that he kept some distance from the enlisted men he liked to 'keep things as relaxed and informal as possible.' He also found Ruby's warmth and womanly presence to be something that he himself more and more looked forward to. He couldn't see Ruby's face in the darkness but he could feel her closeness and her perfume was deliciously heavy. "You're shivering, we'll be there soon, hold on."

Meanwhile, her ever-practical friend and neighbour, Norma believed in making her own sunshine and whilst her Reg was away fighting then her girls were her sunshine. She didn't spend a lot of time trying to make sense of the world around her, her aim was to keep the girls as contented and as happy as she could each day.

Norma and her daughters liked nothing more than escaping the present reality at the cinema. There were many cinemas around at these times and even their small town boasted of having two. Initially, the Government had wanted to keep places of entertainment closed for safety at the beginning of the war but this decision was very unpopular. Norma didn't allow herself to dwell too much on the 'what if's,' her way of getting through was to carry on as best she could, after all, she believed what would happen would happen and staying in and hiding would be tantamount to giving in and letting the Nazis win, 'and that's not going to happen' she would affirm to herself as she washed her dishes.

Norma was amongst the many who believed that life should be carried on as normal as much as possible and her girls eagerly agreed with their mum. Norma loved the Hollywood glamour and the girls enjoyed the comedies and laughed out loud at the cartoons. Norma justified the sometimes twice-weekly visits because the tickets were cheap and less than a shilling. The magic and glamour cheered them all up immensely and there wasn't much else to spend their money on with everything being rationed.

Inevitably they would watch the propaganda films and the newsreels which were created by the Government to inform and lift their spirits. Norma would listen intently because she didn't know where Reg was fighting. He'd left for goodness knows where after a surprise two nights leave and she hadn't heard from him in six months. She did find some consolation in the fact that she hadn't received the dreaded telegram though, telling herself that 'she would cross that bridge if ever she came to it.'

Norma would look keenly at the newsreels hoping to get a sighting of Reg in the streams of marching soldiers embarking and disembarking onto the ships, although she knew that a sighting of her 'old man' was very unlikely. But for the time being taking care of their four daughters kept her 'on an even keel,' keeping them fed and healthy and safe was enough to be going on with for now.

Each night as dusk fell and the sirens wailed Norma's heart would beat ten to the dozen but she kept a calm demeanour so as not to panic her girls. As the war carried on the raids had stepped up and inside her, the fear was rising. Up till now, she had been able to present a confident front with the help of a sneaky Woodbine or two if she could get hold of them.

Reg had always made it clear that he didn't like a woman to smoke, "It's most unladylike" he would mutter when he saw a woman pass him in the street with a cigarette in her mouth.

"But they all smoke in the movies Reg." Norma would laugh.

"Well that's in blinking Hollywood and they are not my wife." He would huff, sticking his chest out possessively.

"Well, what he didn't know wouldn't hurt him" Norma would state firmly as she lit up.

She'd made the sole decision to bring the girls back home and she sometimes wondered whether this had been wise. At the time she had made the only choice that she felt she could when she had visited and had seen the conditions that the girls were placed in. It had made her heart sicken the day that the youngest had been wrenched from her arms and hastily put on the train with her three sisters. She had sobbed all the way home but she had reassured herself that they would settle in, they were good girls after all.

But her surprise visit had revealed fretting

children who were clearly a nuisance to the elderly family that had been authorised to take them in. With heart pounding she had stood her ground and arms folded across her ample breast she had presented a formidable presence. Standing in front of the subdued girls she had ordered the eldest to "Sort out your things I'm taking you home," and she had, on the next train.

.   They had all sat together laughing with relief, eating the bloater paste sandwiches that she'd taken originally for them to have with the picnic that she had planned. Well, they were having their picnic, on the 'blinking train.' They all looked scrawny and the girls ate ravenously.

"Bloody cheek," she said to herself, "telling me that I can't take my own girls home, well I soon showed them stuck up noodles" she smiled smugly.

Suddenly a deafening crash broke into Norma's wandering thoughts! The house shook and the girls screamed out "Mum, mum" and Norma trembled as she gathered her precious family into the comfort of her arms.

She wasn't sure how much protection this Morrison shelter would give them but it had a solid steel top and the mesh at the sides would keep out some of the flying debris.

"Hold tight my darlings, it's just Jerry getting a bit close that's all."

The eldest girl cried out "Mum, I want dad."

"Be brave, I won't let anyone hurt you, remember your dad is out there fighting for us all, he'll give them what for" she soothed.

Clutching her Crucifix she whispered a prayer

and the girls joined in. "Dear father God, please keep us and our Dad safe."

Norma tried to shield her girls with her body, dreading that what she feared would come to pass. Crouched together, trying to keep warm because it was bitterly cold. Norma felt a tickle on her face and hastily brushed it away, thinking that it was a spider, she'd never liked creepy crawlies! Incredulously she was presented with a dark pair of beady, button-like eyes and twitching whiskers.

"A Mouse!" she cried in surprise. He's obviously been startled out of his comfortable nest too! She hastily nudged him away, she didn't want the girls screaming and panicking right at this moment. Now was not the time to worry. Norma pushed her fears to the back of her mind. That's how she coped. Tomorrow morning she would look out onto the street at the damage, and she'd find the mouse trap!

CHAPTER 3.

Eliza dropped her tools when she heard the sirens, she could already hear the familiar drone of the fighter engines overhead. Running over to the shelter she looked up and thought that she could make out the enemy planes. Usually, they had more of a warning but tonight 'they were almost on top of them.' The foreman shouted, "Get down quick chaps."

"Lord help us, I think we are in for it tonight" someone whispered.

It was fresh in their minds about the factory that had been flattened the week before with over a hundred workers lives lost. The Newsreels hadn't mentioned the town by name but some of the present workers had family that had been killed or injured in the air raid, word got around.

Alternative sites were always quickly found and requisitioned. Nothing was allowed to stop the essential war production. The risk was known by all; it was always the important industrial and manufacturing areas that got the worst of it. But now strategic bombing of civilian populations was involved too in an effort to destroy morale. Eliza and her friends found that it had the opposite effect.

Eliza thought of her boys, hoping that they were safe in bed and escaping the worst of the raid. Her feet were cold and she couldn't stop shaking. Her thoughts wondered to Thomas. It was so long ago when she would sit on his knee in their big old armchair by the fire. She remembered how she used to tuck her feet under his long legs to keep them warm. It was so long ago when he used to carry her across the cold scullery floor and she would laughingly cling onto his shirt as he carried her up the stairs to their bedroom. She thought of her Tom with his cheek and his charm, she smiled at his kindness and tenderness towards her. "Where are you Tom" she whispered.

On other nights the workers would pass the time in the shelter playing a game of cards. But this night she had been uneasy. Coming into work Eliza had felt an air of menace all around her and she'd found it difficult to concentrate and to settle into her usual routine.

Eliza felt a rush of air, suddenly she found herself in total blackness and the air around her was hot and smoky. Someone shouted, "We've got to get out."

Eliza felt strong arms pulling her up, feeling dazed she murmured, "Have I been asleep?"

"Come on duck we've got to take a chance."

Eliza was half dragged through the rubble. Her overalls clung to her wet legs and as she looked down she saw that she was covered in blood and she screamed.

The factory had been hit, the fire was fierce and the shelter had caved in from the nearby blast. How long had she been unconscious?

The raid had finished, leaving carnage. She looked up at the indigo sky, at the flames reaching higher and higher. Eliza clung onto Jimmy as they scrambled through the debris.

"Don't look duck, just hold onto me and keep going."

There was little left of Harold's and Violet's home now. The windows had been blown in and Florae the pig had run off screaming in terror. Luckily Rufus was stabled in a nearby barn and hadn't been harmed directly by the bombing thank goodness.

The elderly couple, accompanied by their terrified Labrador, Scoffer, had taken to the safety of the 'Bogey hole' under the stairs at the first sound of the sirens. In the darkness they had listened to the bombs whistling down, saying little, lost in their own inner monologue. Harold glanced over at Violet, occasionally squeezing her hand, wanting to comfort her but not able to find the words.

Violet was thinking back in time to the day when both of her sons had gone off together, smart in their khaki and eager for adventure. She pondered, "Was there a future for them? What would that involve? Would they survive?"

Eric had always led the way when they had been toddlers. Her sons had been born just 18 months apart and Clive had been happy to follow his brother in all of their play. They shared a liking for sport and fishing like their Grandfather and she smiled as she remembered how proud the boys had been when they brought their catch home for tea. Carrying their prize in front of them they would hold the fish up for inspection before dropping it into the sink.

"Had a few bites mum," "Going to cook it for us?" they would ask, beaming because they knew that their mum didn't like to gut and prepare the fish. It was one thing that she could never get used to; even though the fish was fresh she just hated the stare of the glutinous eyeballs.

"It's okay mum, give us the knife, we'll soon have it sorted out" they would laugh.

"Such good boys" she mused.

Scoffer whimpered besides her and she held him tightly, finding his warmth comforting.

Smiling she thought back to the day when she had opened the door to the sight of Scoffer racing past her with a squashed meat pie in his mouth closely followed by Harold, red in the face and with his hair sticking up vertically with a smear of gravy on his forehead.

"What the heck?" she had cried," For goodness sakes Harold what's going on?"

"I'd just turned my back to get my brown sauce and the little bugger jumped up and pinched it."

How she had laughed. Scoffer had always been quick off the mark and had never had any reservations about helping himself to a tasty treat. Harold's sulking had just made it more ridiculously funny.

"You're not so quick now days are you pet" she whispered into his golden softness.

"Sorry love?" Harold asked.

"Nothing Harold, just reminiscing."

She sighed, "Enough of the past."

Violet had imagined their future being happy and comfortable, Hadn't they all thought that WW1 would be the last of all world wars?

Arthur Pickering had been kept busy during

the night. As soon as darkness fell he donned his white helmet, slung his gas mask over his shoulder and set off for another shift as a Fire warden. Finding his way around in the imposed blackout had been unsettling initially but he had soon became accustomed to it, although he knew from experience that it could pose many hazards if a person became too complacent.

Arthur had managed to carefully climb up the iron staircase onto the warehouse rooftop so that he would be able to have a good view of any trouble. Sometimes he would spot a careless light showing from up here, sometimes he would spot a fire and send for fire engines or ambulance, and he never really knew what was in front of him. Sometimes he would be on the spot to help douse a small fire or help rescue those who were trapped under rubble. Arthur wiped the sweat from his brow, tonight had been hell.

Harold and Violet's roof had caved in. Arthur and others on the scene fought their way through the still smouldering debris, not knowing who or what they would find. The enemy planes had now flown over and the night seemed deadly quiet, all sound muffled as a light drizzle of rain fell. Arthur realised that this was Harold and Violet's place and remembered that they would have been sheltering under the stairs.

His heart pounding he shouted out, "Give us a hand; they will be under the stairs."

Harold and Violet were not on their own in believing that under the stairs was the safest part of the house because of its load-bearing structure.

Arthur knew that if they had 'copped' a direct hit then nothing would save them but he hoped that they hadn't had a direct hit and there may be a chance to get them out.

Pushing their way through they found the cupboard door had been blown off and the stairs had collapsed inwards. Crawling under the debris the rescuers pushed their way through slowly.

Harold and Violet were in each other's arms covered in dust and for one heart-stopping moment Arthur thought that they had 'Both copped it.' Their old dog, Scoffer, whimpered and started to lick Violet's face.

A dazed Violet responded to the warm wetness of Scoffer's tongue and looking into the light of the torch she called out, "Oh, my Gaud are we glad to see you."

Trying to calm the frantic dog she turned to Harold, "Are you alright duck?" She prodded him.

Harold was still slumped forward and trickles of blood oozed from under his hairline. He looked as if he was asleep. Violet shook him, her heart was pounding and she fell onto him clumsily in her panic. Harold opened one eye.

"Careful old girl, mind the family jewels!"

Arthur Pickering smiled in relief.

"Ah! So all three of you are in here then!"

Joanie Pickering Stretched out her legs rubbed her aching arms and brushed her hair back from her face. She had became accustomed to Arthur being gone all night, busy with his duties of a Fire warden, and she knew that it would have been useless to try and persuade him that, "it was all a bit much for him now at his age." It was just a case of 'putting up and shutting up' and smiling a welcome when he finally arrived home, usually 'the worse for wear.'

"I'm so cold, time for a cuppa and a look at the damage" she murmured. Joanie stiffly climbed up from the Anderson shelter to ground level and looked out.

The house was standing but others at the far end of the street were not so lucky. Fire was raging and the flames were shooting up into the dawn sky where the engineering factory had been, just 20-minutes walk from where she now stood. Joanie let herself into her kitchen and filled the kettle and as she did so she wondered. Was her Arthur safe? Had Frances and Eliza been on the night shift at the factory? How had Lizzie managed, had she slept under her stairs again? Were Norma and the girls safe? Had Ruby stayed at the base? The kettle whistled cutting into her thoughts and making her jump. Joanie filled up the big blue teapot, glad that she still had plenty of wood for her stove.

A chair tumbled over behind her and Midnight shot out from under her table and stretched himself in front of the stove for warmth. "Hello puss, how long have you been under there? Have you been hiding under there all night?" Midnight gave Joanie a good, long, look and meowed loudly. Joanie leant forward and stroked him feeling glad of the company and she asked him gently "Want a drink." She gave him a saucer of hot tea with a splash of milk. His Whiskers twitching Midnight sniffed it and then lapped it up greedily. As Joanie moved forward to stroke him she noticed with surprise that her hands were shaking. Midnight allowed Joanie to stroke him whilst he licked the milk from her hands with his rough tongue. Suddenly he raised his head and his eyes darkened. There were voices outside; he arched his back and shot forward, darting out of the kitchen and through the back door.

Arthur stood framed in the doorway, his clothes were covered in dust and his face was blackened. Joanie jumped up. "You gave me a start Arthur, goodness, look at you."

"Got some company love" he replied quietly.

Harold and Violet were standing just behind Arthur.

"We've been bombed out Joanie" Violet whispered. Joanie stretched out her arms and held them both.

"Come in the warmth, come on in."

Scoffer shot forward, keen to be included and Joanie laughingly petted him.

Joanie settled them both in comfy armchairs in front of her stove and they drank a cup of tea with 'a bit of the hard stuff' gratefully. As she gazed at the elderly couple she was filled with compassion. They looked so fragile and she wondered what would happen to them now. Of course, someone would take them in but to lose your home at their time of life was particularly tough. Joanie tucked a blanket around each of them and they all sat in the warmth and the quiet, the clock ticked and Harold dropped off to sleep, snoring softly as the Golden Labrador rested at his feet.

Arthur was gone from the kitchen for a while and then came back in struggling with a large, bulky sack which he then took out to the outhouse.

"What have you got in there Arthur?" Joanie

cried in alarm.

Harold and Violet looked up, then at Arthur and then Joanie, not saying a word. "Well, what is it?" Joanie asked again, intrigued.

"It's the pig love; she copped it I'm afraid, looks like we will all have our bacon early." He announced.

"Well, I never" Joanie stared. Harold and Violet stared. Arthur laughed and they all joined in loudly, laughing until they cried.

Back on their grandfather's farm Eliza's boys had been woken by the drone of the fighter's engines overhead. A voice called up the stairs.

"Charlie, Michael, get up, quickly."

The twins knelt up on their bed; both were keen to see the action outside. They saw a glow in the sky in the distance and shouted to each other in excitement.

Sam grabbed the 6-year-old twins and put one under each of his arms and they clung on around their grandfather's neck as he clambered down the dark stairs into the kitchen. He dropped them down in a bundle of arms and legs onto the sofa and called out, "Kathleen, quick, I think we are in for it tonight, can you get some blankets and candles, we will all need to get down into the shelter pretty sharpish."

They all huddled together in the darkness, the twins peeping from under their blankets in fright at the flickering shadows made by the candles. There were a couple of old mattresses down there and Kathleen had made up makeshift beds for the boys, but the twins had climbed onto their grandparents' laps needing the extra closeness and security that this provided after the initial excitement had worn off. Grandfather and Michael were cuddled under one blanket and grandma and Charlie wrapped tightly under another eiderdown. Sam and Kathleen were both lost in their own thoughts, neither mentioning their shared dread that their daughter Eliza would 'be in the thick of it.' Eventually, the boys had managed to drop back off to sleep and Kathleen gazed at them fondly thinking wistfully "If only their mother was here with us."

The farm was a good way from the small town and factories but Kathleen knew the damage that a stray bomb could cause. They'd had a close call a few weeks ago when an enemy aircraft had crashed into a nearby barn and burst into flames. The German bomber had been damaged and flying off course, and helpers had not been able to get near because of the heat and explosions.

Kathleen shuddered as she remembered the screams of the crew who although they had managed to survive the impact of the crash found them to be terrifyingly trapped in a raging burning hell. The wreckage still remained to remind them of the terribleness of war and Kathleen couldn't help but wonder that these young men were somebody's sons and husbands. Sam became impatient when she voiced her distress; he had glared his disapproval and stomped off to feed the livestock muttering into his woolly donkey jacket.

"You don't know the half of what these Jerries are capable of woman, if those Jerries had survived they'd have thought nothing of finishing us off in our beds, the stories I hear in the pub are shocking, those Nazis are capable of anything." He'd sighed.

Kathleen had for once answered him back, refusing to be on the defensive,

"Aye, but It's hard to see anyone suffer such a violent ending, even Germans are human beings after all." She'd slammed the door after him.

Kathleen still heard their screams in her sleep.

Kathleen thought back to the last time when Eliza had visited and she and her father, well, they'd had words. Eliza's flat refusal to stay and help out on their small farm had caused Sam to feel hurt and angry. He'd been at a loss to understand his only daughter's stubbornness.

"You're a married woman Eliza" he'd protested, "Tom would want you to be here with us and the boys. We could do with the help now that two of the farm hands have been called up, and you would be out of the worst of it."

Eliza had held her ground, insisting "I know dad but I'm needed where I am, they need every pair of hands that they can get, you know how important it is that the women help out in the factories now that most of the young men have been called up."

She'd felt trapped, it was difficult to explain without hurting her parents, but she was a married woman and the thought of living under her father's authoritarian rule was not an option. She'd married a man that was easy going and kind, a man who loved women, maybe a bit too much, she'd thought at times. Thomas treated her as an equal and he used to laugh at her need for fripperies and her flirty ways.

"No, as long as the boys were safe then I know that he will be accepting of my choice and be pleased with the wages that I am saving for when this is all over." she'd repeated firmly. Sam had reluctantly accepted the state of affairs and Kathleen had been very relieved.

Sam gazed out over his land, he pulled his cap forward against the cold, the 'all clear' had sounded just after dawn and he'd whispered to Kathleen to stay put in the shelter and he'd eased the still sleeping Michael down and left the shelter to check on the cottage and his livestock.

The red glowing in the distance lit up the silhouette of the oak trees against the sky. The air was heavy and still and the usual dawn chorus of the birds had been silenced. A dog barked in the distance, yes! The cottage was still standing.

Sam tried to swallow, feeling a lump in his throat and tears stinging his eyes. He was a self-made man and the living that he's managed to carve out for himself and his family was everything to him. He was a man of few words and found it difficult to express his feelings and emotions and he felt that Eliza 'took against him' because of this. His wife Kathleen had known him since they were children and she understood that he cared for his family and she was able to appreciate that he was a good provider and that she could always rely on him. She mostly forgave his seeming harshness but Eliza was a 'different kettle of fish.' He sighed and moved on to the barn, all seemed to be as it should be.

Kathleen shook the boys gently, waiting for Sam to return to hopefully tell them that all was safe. Kathleen had lost two of her sisters in an air raid when their munitions factory had taken a direct hit. She shivered, feeling an overwhelming sadness engulf her as tears streamed down her face. So much Death and destruction everywhere, "When would all of this end?"

She trembled as the raw emotions and the sense of loss coursed through her whole being. "Please God, please let her Eliza be safe, please don't take her as well." she cried out.

Suddenly a figure stooped in the doorway of the shelter, it was her Sam.

"Come on duck, come on boys, home's still standing."

They made their way back to the solid welcoming cottage and the boys pushed their way into the kitchen. Michael was fractious and hungry too.

"I want mum gran, when is she coming to see us?"

Kathleen looked up at Sam; stifling her emotions she spoke briskly to hide her fear.

"Wash your hands and face lads and sit at the table, mum will be here soon."

"I'll put the wireless on" stated Sam firmly when he had noted his wife's tear-stained face. "Let's have a bit of music to cheer us up" and he'd gently squeezed her hand.

CHAPTER 4.

It was 5.30 am, time for Frances to set off for work. She stretched her long legs out in front of her and looked around the kitchen for the cat. Midnight jumped onto his mistresses' lap and curled into her softness.

"Where did you get to then? Blimey, your tail's all scorched; let me have a look at you" she cried. "Crikey, you stink of smoke Midnight; you look like you've been pulled through a hedge backwards." Frances laughed.

Midnight took exception to the examination of his tail and jumping down he darted out into the yard and he was soon off on his daily scavenging and hunting adventures again.

Frances pulled her coat around her tightly and pushed her sardine paste sandwiches into her coat pocket. Wrapping a thick woollen scarf around her throat and shoulders she glanced around the room quickly before setting off for a brisk walk. Knowing that Eliza would be home soon from her shift Frances left a saucepan of porridge on the stove and some scraps for Midnight in his bowl. Sighing she realised that she was starting the day feeling weary before she even began her long 12-hour shift.

"Oh, if only this war would soon come to an end" she whispered to the empty room, "I wish I could have Mr Winston Churchill's faith in the

British people's ability to get through all of this. This war is causing a lot of people to question their beliefs and the old way of doing things," she murmured.

Lifting the latch she stepped out into the early morning, the air was thick with ash and smoke and she wondered nervously what sights would greet her.

Frances didn't get far before Eliza stumbled into her followed closely by Jimmy.

"It's gone Frances, the factory, the shelter, the whole lot. Jimmy dragged me out of the shelter. Not many made it Frances" Eliza gasped. "It was so black and the smoke was choking me but Jimmy grabbed hold of me and pulled me through. Jimmy stayed with me at the church hall while the WRVS fixed us up and gave us a cuppa."

Frances stared at Eliza's bloodied overalls in dismay. She couldn't move or think for a moment.

"Frances, it's not mine, it's some other poor blighters. They gave me a couple of aspirins and my legs are grazed from the rubble but I will be alright. I'm just a bit shaky that's all, I think I fainted."

Jimmy stepped forward.

"It's all gone Frances, there's nothing left, nothing standing. You might as well take your coat off. Damn the Jerries and damn this war." He shouted angrily.

Jimmy normally gentle in manner in speech and bearing hastily wiped a trickle of blood that was oozing from a bandage wrapped around his forehead. His thick brown curly hair was bloodied and dusty. Frances shot forward, suddenly jumping into action.

"No, leave it Frances, it will settle down, I'm off to see what I can do to help out, there's still a lot buried under rubble and the army lads need some help digging out any survivors" Jimmy asserted hastily.

"I should go and help at the church Hall; I've done my first aid course." Frances insisted.

"No Frances, Eliza's had a 'bad do,' she was unconscious for a while. Stay with her for now and I'll catch up with you both later." Jimmy rushed out leaving the door wide open to the cold morning air.

The ambulance sirens could be heard in the distance and Eliza shivered. Eliza's legs trembled and she slumped down onto the sofa suddenly feeling nauseous and icy cold.

"The bodies are still there Frances, laying in the dust and the rubble. So many of our workmates are gone, so many of them, so much blood" she sobbed, rocking back and forwards.

"There are so many injured at the church hall. I saw dead babies Frances." she shuddered. "I sat in the corner, watching whilst the injured were brought in on stretchers; the dead were just put behind a curtain until there was time for them to be identified. But there were others drinking tea and nattering! I wanted to scream at them, don't you realise that I've left my friends buried under that lot, how can you be drinking tea?" She sobbed.

"Come on then love, let's get you out of these clothes and into bed. I'll bring you something up that will help you settle." Frances soothed.

"It's how people seem to get by Eliza, we are all frightened and some only seem to manage by pushing everything away. Things aren't looking good for our boys at the moment and we don't know what anyone else has been through, try not to judge."

"I know Fran, I'm sorry, I'm just in shock."

Frances helped Eliza up the stairs and into bed. Regretting her harsh words she took her a cup of strong sweet tea and tucked her in.

"Sorry I snapped love, I don't know what comes over me sometimes lately" she apologised. "Sweet dreams."

"I know Frances, we are all feeling the strain" Eliza smiled. "I'm so tired, I hope I do dream, dream of an escape from this hell."

Frances sat by her stove, deep in thought and reflection. How she longed to see her Joseph.

"If I could only one more gaze into his dear loving face" she whispered.

Frances still hadn't heard any more news about Joseph since the day that she had opened the telegram reporting him missing in action and that was two years ago! She had read and reread the first letters that he had sent her, always waiting for the postman and being disappointed.

Was Joseph dead? Laying somewhere, crumpled in the earth, broken and forgotten? But she was sure that if he was dead then she would know in some part of her she argued.

"No Joe, never forgotten" she cried.

She swallowed the anger that welled up from deep inside her.

"Enough Frances, what good will bitterness do, it will just make you more miserable."

But at times she imagined that she could feel Joseph's spirit watching her. She was sure at these times that he hadn't left her and that he was alive somewhere trying to reach her. Or was it like Lizzie had explained, "In death we do not end in the depths of matter, our spirit carries on. Our earthly experiences are only temporary Frances" she would advise kindly.

"I hope you are right Lizzie" she whispered.

She stared at the photograph of Joseph that stood on the mantelpiece.

"Joseph, my darling love, I'm still patiently waiting."

Lizzie burst in, sweating and breathless.

"The factory has gone, the shelter's gone. Oh Gaud, Ruby's not home either. I saw Eliza at the church hall with Jimmy. Is she back safe Frances? Oh, I'm all in lather" she gasped.

"She's having a rest Lizzie, Cup of tea? You look done in."

"I just left Norma and the girls. The blast blew the windows clean out. They are being boarded up just now. They are just being cleaned up a bit, none of them is hurt thank the Lord. Susan, the poor little mite had wet herself with fright. Heaven help us all, she just shot out into the road and I ran as fast as my old legs would take me. I just managed to catch hold of her and then I slipped on my backside. There was glass everywhere. I stayed with them until things calmed down a bit" Lizzie blustered.

"You've ripped your trousers Lizzie, I can see your red bloomers" Frances giggled.

Lizzie sat herself down quickly and throwing her head back she pushed her dark hair away from her flushed face.

"I will have that cuppa please love, I am parched. While you are about it have one with me and I'll have a little look in your cup."

They sat together, each lost in their own thoughts. Lizzie was thinking back to the way Jimmy had hovered around Eliza at the church hall. Frances was taking a quiet moment in the calm. The clock ticked steadily, Frances fancied that it seemed to be ticking louder and louder. Lizzie dozed and Frances hummed.

Upstairs Eliza woke and stretched. Thomas's photograph had fallen onto the mat at the side of the bed and Eliza leant forward and clutched his wonderful likeness to her heart. She wondered where his ship was now, "is he missing me as I am missing him? Or is he enjoying other female company, perhaps making up for the everyday dangers by drinking heavily and getting into fights again."

Thomas was handsome, with his stocky muscular build and pleasing cheeky personality he had always managed to attract the interest of other females. He knew that he had a way with women and he was always ready with sweet talk and smiles. Wasn't this what had attracted her to Thomas in the beginning?

Eliza had first met Thomas when she and a friend were queuing to watch a movie at the Picture House. Thomas was with a group of friends immediately behind them and sensing his gaze she turned and gazed at a very attractive lad who stared back at her. He had looked straight into her eyes and smiled his winning smile. Walking up to her he asked if Eliza and her friend Doris would like to join them. Eliza felt an instant attraction to the young man with the blue twinkling eyes and she laughed.

"Maybe we will, maybe we won't" she

answered looking him up and down. He had an air of a seaman with his ruddy, weathered complexion and navy polo neck jumper.

"Oh come on Eliza" Doris urged, "We won't have to pay" she whispered.

"All right then, but no funny business, my dad's warned me about you sailor types with a girl in every port."

"I'm not asking you to marry me ducks, just asking you both if you'd like to join us to watch a film and share some good company with us lads before we report back to sea." Thomas replied hopefully.

That had been the beginning of a whirlwind courtship, then a hasty marriage and the birth of twin boys.

Thomas had in fact been taking leave from his post in the Merchant Navy when she had met him that day. During his leave, he would collect her from the farm on his Triumph motorbike wearing a black heavy leather jacket and dark cord trousers and heavy boots. Eliza loved to ride pillion, pressing her face into the softness .of the leather jacket and holding tight to his heavy buckled belt she would escape the drudgery of the farm, and Thomas had made her heart skip!

Eliza would rush out to meet him, wearing a turquoise silk headscarf to keep her hair tidy and a warm woollen jacket with the collar turned up to keep out the cold and the damp, and of course her evening in Paris perfume and her Elizabeth Arden red lipstick. She felt like she was in the movies when Thomas roared up to the door to collect her.

Eliza's parents Sam and Kathleen had soon

warmed to Eliza's beau and surprisingly despite Sam's previous strictness he allowed Thomas to collect his daughter on his motorbike and take her to the pictures or a dance. Sam would sit up, smoking on his pipe until they returned but he had made a decision that perhaps it was time to allow his daughter a little freedom and he felt that he could trust 'young Thomas,' he'd taken a liking to him.

Kathleen had also taken Thomas under her motherly wing on hearing that he had been brought up in an orphanage and that he had joined the Merchant Navy at the tender age of 14 years. Thomas's pay had been poor compared to factory workers and Kathleen would feed him up with fresh eggs and butter and cheese to make up for the lack of fresh food that he was served with at sea. She enjoyed spoiling him, she would have liked a son and she treated Thomas as if he was her own.

The British Merchant Navy were now keeping the country supplied with valuable necessities such as fuel, ammunition and food and both Sam and Kathleen were acutely aware of the very high risk that Thomas faced daily as a seaman in the Merchant Navy in wartime. They were both very proud of him too and of the two lovely grandsons that were so like their daddy in their looks. Kathleen prayed that Thomas would return to them.

Upstairs in her bedroom Eliza gazed at the photograph. She hadn't received any letters from Thomas for a month. She thought back to the conversations between Thomas and Sam when they had discussed their concerns that most merchant ships were not designed to withstand a heavy enemy attack. Sometimes groups of Merchant ships would travel in a convoy and be provided with an escort of warships but this didn't prevent heavy losses. Thomas and Sam were very aware that the risk to life was high.

Eliza shuddered, "So am I."

When the war had broken out Eliza had taken on work in an engineering factory in the small town nearby and she had quickly settled in and made friends with the other workers there, some of them arriving from Europe and some being recent British evacuees from the Channel Isles. With Thomas away at sea Eliza had been only too pleased to share a house with Frances.

Eliza had found that her relationship with her dad was tolerable when they weren't in each other's company too often. She found it to be an impossible strain to live under the same roof, finding her father's bombastic temperament and refusal to accept his increasing years, exhausting in the extreme. His need to control every level of the family routine caused many arguments between them and when Eliza lapsed in her efforts to 'keep the peace' for her mum's sake she would observe Sam's hidden vulnerability and his now physical frailty and feel terribly frustrated that once again she wasn't able to override her need to assert her adulthood. Either way, giving in to his sometimes abruptness or arguing against it just left her feeling terribly upset with herself and guilty about putting her mum 'in the middle' again. She couldn't disagree with Kathleen's justification that Sam was a good provider and that

Eliza had never gone without anything, but Eliza was a 'different cut' to her mother that was why she and Thomas had been and still were so right for each other.

The boys had stayed at the farm with Sam and Kathleen and as they were both under 5 years she knew that they wouldn't be evacuated yet. Besides she had heard stories about some of the evacuated children being so dreadfully unhappy that they had run away. "No, I will cross that bridge when I come to it." She had asserted.

Eliza had insisted that the factory pay was good, in fact, better than her husband's pay and besides she "Wanted to do her bit." Sam had reluctantly agreed and Kathleen was happy to "Take on the boys."

But just now Sam had heard about the heavy raid on the town and he planned to get in to see his daughter as soon as he could get away from the farm. This morning the lads had been fretful and they were missing their mum.

"Right Kath, I'm going to see the animals and then I'm off to see our daughter" Sam called up the stairs "Be good boys for your gran."

Sam stood in the doorway in goggles and Thomas's jacket. He had driven as best as he could into town on the motorcycle, over the rubble and past the fires still burning and the wreckage of the houses. The dust and smoke had caused his throat to dry up and the goggles had not prevented the acrid smoke stinging his eyes which were now red raw.

Coughing and sputtering he pulled his helmet off. "Hello ladies, can I come in then?"

Eliza jumped off the bed and ran down the stairs on hearing the motorbike engine. Her heart jumped in her chest.

"Thomas?" she cried hopefully.

"No, it's your dad, pack a bag Eliza; you're coming home with me." Sam replied.

Eliza didn't argue, with resignation she started back up the stairs to gather a few of her clothes and 'what not's.' She didn't worry too much about her work knowing that the factory would soon be set up again once a suitable location was found. Besides, she had a hankering to try for a driving job, maybe on the buses or ambulances this time. Women were driving tractors and tanks and she'd even heard of women piloting planes about the country. Eliza was spirited and adventurous and didn't plan on staying on the farm for too long, wearing dungarees and making rabbit pie!

"This war is an escape for us women and I am going to take full advantage of the opportunities that it brings" Eliza muttered to herself as she ran back upstairs to grab Thomas's photo.

But for now she was ready to return with her dad and to spend some time with her boys and her mum. Feeling very vulnerable and shaken even her dad's tetchiness was welcome at this moment.

Eliza knew that Sam was a good man even though his controlling manner with her when she was growing into a woman had been difficult to live with. However, right at this moment, his protectiveness was just what she needed. She needed the love from her family, security, her beautiful sons, and familiar surroundings. She hoped that going home would fill the painful emptiness that threatened to overwhelm her since the raid and her being trapped in the shelter.

For one glorious moment when she had heard the roar of the motorbike, she had thought Thomas was home.

"My Thomas, My love" she whispered.

Sam glanced at her impatiently.

Eliza and Sam set off within the hour because Sam wanted to be gone before dusk and the blackout, these winter days it was dark at 4 pm.

Lizzie and Frances had hugged them both, wishing them a safe journey, for one never knew these days if a simple "Tara" would be the last goodbye. Lizzie gave Eliza a warm multi-striped scarf each for the boys which she had knitted from unpicked sweaters and a red knitted tea cosy for Kathleen. Lizzie had a lot of time on her hands and she knew that Kathleen had her work cut out with her grandsons and the farm.

CHAPTER 5.

Lizzie stirred, she'd dropped off to sleep and Frances was sitting next to the wireless, humming along with 'The Forces Sweetheart' Vera Lynn.

"The tea is cold Lizzie, don't jump up, you were fast asleep, I'll just pop to 'the lavvy' and make us a fresh brew, I won't be long." Frances said smiling.

Lizzie dragged her self back into wakefulness. She'd been thinking back on her life and fell asleep. She'd been thinking way back to her childhood, to the time when she'd met Jack and of their life together, of her little girl who'd she'd lost early.

Lizzie had been a widow for the past 10 years. Jack, her husband, well, he'd liked a tipple and on occasions when he had been a younger man he'd not been averse to giving Lizzie a push or a slap if she'd 'overstepped the mark' and answered him back.

"He'd always been a grafter," she mused, insisting that "No wife of mine needs to go out to work."

Lizzie had filled her life being a busy housewife and mother to their daughter Dorothy Anne whom Jack idolised. They had lost Dorothy Anne to this world at the young age of 6 years following a seven-week battle with whooping cough which had developed into Pneumonia. Jack and

Lizzie's marriage had never really recovered following the death of their only daughter.

Jack started to visit the pub on his way home from the Foundry finding it hard to come home from work and no longer be greeted by Dorothy Anne jumping up and down and pestering for the mints that he had in his pocket or demanding to be held upside down by her feet with Jack crying "Ere, let's have a look at what's in your pockets" in his scary 'Policeman's voice.'

Lizzie had mourned her daughter in her own quiet way, walking up to the cemetery each afternoon come rain or shine to put a sweet by the headstone or perhaps a little bunch of daisies or buttercups when they were in season. At first she couldn't bear to think of her being alone until she had a dream of Dorothy Ann telling her "I'm alright mum, I'm with other children and kind 'grown-ups' who are lovely and I'm all well now and gran says to tell you please don't come down to the cemetery every day getting wet because I'm really not there."

Lizzie had accepted the way her marriage was, many of the women around had a more to worry about than a husband that spent time in the pub after work and came home to eat his dinner and then fall asleep in the chair.

She remembered her father's words to her when she and Jack had started 'walking out.'

"No good will ever come of this Lizzie, he's a good enough chap but he's not right for you."

Lizzie's father knew that his daughter was a sensitive girl, strange in some ways and Jack was a 'rough and ready' type and he didn't believe that he would be able to give his daughter the gentleness and understanding that she needed.

But Jack had courted her relentlessly with passion and determination and she had been flattered. He always had money in his pocket and having inherited money from his late father he was able to put down a small deposit on a terraced house. Jack had always promised that if she would marry him then he would always take care of her.

Lizzie had let Jack sweep her off her feet and they had honeymooned in Blackpool and she had thought how lucky she was.

Lizzie's father had been a 'Chapelgoer' and he had struggled with Lizzie's 'gift' as her mother had liked to call it. When his wife had died of Tuberculosis when Lizzie was only 11 years old he had found himself at a loss to understand his daughter's stories of nighttime 'shiny visitors' and her acute sensitivity that often caused him embarrassment.

When Lizzie told him that she didn't like a certain person because they had "a funny colour around them and they make me feel sad" he would stare at her, lost for words.

Lizzie's friends would laugh at her behaviour nervously and call her "daft" but as they all grew up together they had begun to have a respect for their strange friend and her warnings.

Just a short while after her marriage one morning Lizzie had rushed around to her Father's house after Jack had left for the Foundry and asked him to stay away from work. He had shrugged and shook his head, ignoring her insistent pleas he had become cross and slammed out of the house.

That evening he hadn't returned, instead there had been a knock on Jack's door at 8 pm and Jack had stood outside the kitchen in the yard, whispering with a man who smelt strongly of whiskey.

"Jack, who is it? Ask them in" she had called out. It wasn't like Jack to keep a person on the step Lizzie worried.

Jack shut the door behind him and sat Lizzie down. She knew before he told her!

"Jack, what's happened to dad?"

Lizzie's father had been crushed in an accident at the factory.

Lizzie was just 18 years old then, just newly married and she had buried her father three weeks later.

She smiled, she had been thankful for the home that Jack had bought for them and she knew that in his way he had loved her. He had never looked at another woman during their marriage and she thanked her lucky stars for that.

Jack's fondness for rum and cigarettes had eventually brought on a massive fatal heart attack. Lizzie had him buried in a plot next to their daughter Dorothy Ann. Jack had been a good father to his daughter and she knew in her heart that they would be united in spirit. She had gained comfort from this.

Lizzie had taken female lodgers in after her husband's death to help her make 'ends meet.'

Lizzie had also earned a steady few bob with her skills of reading the tea leaves and looking into her crystal ball. She thought back to her chapel-going father and hoped that he would be more understanding of her gift now that he had passed over to spirit.

Frances bustled back in the room, carrying a fresh pot of tea. Now fully awake and back in the present Lizzie rubbed her arms and tidied the wisps of hair, checking her rollers were still in place.

She glanced over at Frances, sitting opposite.

"Come on then duck, let's drink this cuppa and switch the wireless off and then let's see what we can find."

Lizzie studied Frances's teacup. The silence in the room intensified and Frances waited, noting Lizzie's intense gaze into the delicate blue glazed China teacup. Lizzie glanced up, seemingly staring into open space and then she smiled and looked back into the cup in front of her.

Come on Lizzie, what do you see? Frances urged.

"I think I'm losing my touch Frances, look, at the bottom of the cup."

Frances eagerly looked into the teacup.

"The leaves indicate an unplanned pregnancy." Lizzie announced.

"Lizzie, oh no! It's impossible." Frances gasped, incredulous that Lizzie could say such a thing.

"Only you turned the cup Frances, could maybe mean an unplanned venture, but look near the handle too."

Lizzie murmured then looked up sharply.

"What is it Lizzie, I want to know the truth, please."

The two women were concerned and puzzled. Frances hugged her body tightly and Lizzie stared down at the brown lino, pushing the peg rug around with her slippered feet.

"Well, we need to balance the reading, good and bad against each other Frances. We've got a heart near the handle too."

"A Lover? Lizzie I don't understand, you know me, I haven't been with any bloke since Joseph went missing." Frances protested.

A look of understanding crossed Lizzie's face followed by a fleeting expression of acceptance.

"Don't worry love; there are things that we see sometimes that we can never understand. Come on; let's put the wireless back on. I've had enough of this, the fires going out and I'm blinking cold."

"Oh, right, I'll get some coal in for us, stay and keep me company, will you?" Frances pleaded.

Frances hurried into the yard and began to throw coal into a bucket.

Lizzie sat quietly, gazing out of the back door up to the darkening steel grey sky.

Frances noticed a strange oddness in Lizzie's manner, she was usually so sprightly and confident and tonight Frances thought how frail her elderly friend was becoming.

"What are you doing Lizzie, hoping for inspiration" she joked.

Lizzie smiled hastily. She wasn't going to share the truth that had burst through like the sun suddenly peering from behind a cloud. No, she would keep her epiphany to herself.

That was Eliza's cup, I blinking knew it, that Jimmy didn't have a reputation for being a ladies' man for nothing she thought. I could dearly give him a clout around his ears for being so irresponsible.

"Damned if I know," she answered with a tinge of sadness in her voice." I was away with the fairies I think. You bank the fire up love and I'll nip to Norma's and see if she's got a bit of bread pudding to spare." Lizzie rushed out, glad of a moment to gather her thoughts. That was awkward.

Frances was puzzled and the reading had left her strangely unsettled. Sighing she leant forward and tuned into the Light Programme. She smoothed her fingers along the polished veneer of the wireless which Joseph had proudly presented her with in the early years of their marriage. She was hoping that the BBC would be playing something cheerful, maybe something by one of the popular British singers such as George Formby or Gracie Fields.

Her usual favourite programme was Vera Lynn's very own show called 'Sincerely Yours' and during this broadcast, Vera would read out personal messages between the Forces and their sweethearts.

Just at this moment Frances didn't think that she could bear to listen to any of Vera's hauntingly beautiful lyrics or melodies. She knew that if she heard her usual favourite of "We'll Meet Again" she would dissolve into tears.

Frances thought of her best friend Ruby. Yes, Ruby had acquired a certain reputation which Frances thought was unfair and of which she had decidedly chosen to overlook.

She smiled as she thought back to a couple of evenings ago when they had both sang along together to some of the songs that were played by the Americans at the base. Ruby was very partial to the American Crooners and she knew the lyrics word by word. They had kicked up the kitchen rug and had

'Jitterbugged' around until they collapsed with laughter. Midnight had protested loudly at this strange display of human behaviour.

"I wonder what's happened to Ruby," Frances said quietly to herself.

Frances tried to relax, humming along to the music she waited for Lizzie to return. Leaning forward to turn up the volume Frances knocked the teapot over spilling its contents over the cloth. Jumping up she hastily gathered the crockery together.

"Where's Lizzie gone to? I'll have to make a fresh brew" she sighed. Wasting tea was not her usual practice now that tea was rationed to a few ounces a week.

Relieved that she hadn't smashed any crockery she was rinsing the cups under the tap when she heard voices outside.

Ruby burst into the kitchen followed by a 'Yank' close on her heels.

At the same time, Lizzie swanked in with the bread pudding and bent down to put the wonderful plateful of spicy stodge onto a low table near the stove.

Ruby roared with laughter as Lizzie's red flannel drawers were clearly in view.

With a jolt Lizzie remembered her earlier accident and realised the unsightly presentation that she had made in front of Rubies' guest.

"Oh gaud, I forgot all about my split trousers" and as she straightened up quickly she passed a very loud, rumbling fart!

The American officer accompanying Ruby blushed and politely turned away.

Ruby and Frances couldn't believe their ears; Lizzie's introduction to Ruby's gentleman friend would not be forgotten in a hurry.

Suppressing a giggle Ruby darted forward and hugged Frances and Lizzie, with a merry glint in her eyes she presented the tall very handsome stranger.

"This is First Lieutenant Parker, always the Southern Gentleman! He brought me back from the base."

Frances poured out the tea and handed out the warm bread pudding.

"No coffee I'm afraid" she smiled hesitantly.

"Thank you Ma'am, I've managed to acquire a taste for this British brew since I've been over here and I'm sure it wouldn't be polite to complain about your British custom of tea and cake on our first introduction," the officer answered smoothly as he stared down intently into Frances's flushed face.

What a beauty, thought Lieutenant Parker as he gazed in deep appreciation into Frances's sea green eyes.

Ruby laughed, she was well used to men's reaction when they first met Frances but she was confident of being attractive in her own right. Ruby turned many heads with her assets of rich, russet coloured wavy hair and her curvy figure with everything being, 'just in the right place.'

For all Frances's beauty, Ruby made up for it with her warm heart, her wonderfully evocative singing voice and her confidence and wit. She was not threatened by her friend's ethereal, delicate beauty and she knew that Frances would never be seduced by Lieutenant Parker's fine Southern charm and sophistication. She knew that her friend was one of a kind, that she would always be eternally faithful to her first love and would probably die a widow if Joseph didn't survive.

Ruby worried about Frances's ability to cope if Joseph didn't return, whilst he was missing there was always hope, although Ruby doubted a happy outcome after such a long time. When Ruby had made attempts to prepare Frances for such an outcome Frances's expression would set like granite and she would flounce off, accusing Ruby that "You know nothing, you will never have what me and Joseph have, so please just leave me alone," and Ruby would leave her alone, for the time being anyway. But today Ruby was again concerned, for beneath her friend's delicate pastel pink complexion there were darkening shadows appearing under her eyes which she didn't put down just to shift working and lack of sleep.

"Well, sit down Lieutenant" invited Lizzie, who had noticed John Parker's very obvious appreciation of Frances. She gave him her 'I might seem ancient but there are no bats in my belfry yet' look much to his consternation and Ruby's amusement.

The American officer was very taken with Ruby and had not been aware of rustling any feathers. Unsettled by the challenging stare from the elderly grey haired lady with the steel roller in the front of her hair he concentrated on drinking his cup of strong British tea and tried heroically to eat his way through the strange brown heavy pudding.

"These Yanks, their reputation for being slick and charming is hardly surprising," Lizzie reflected. "Why, he could charm the pants off a Nun!"

She didn't judge Ruby for one minute, life was calling and Ruby wouldn't have her youth forever, besides why should there be one rule for the men and one for the women. Ruby hadn't made any commitments to any of the lads that were away fighting; she knew of her reputation and carried on as she pleased in defiance of it.

Lizzie's view was that none of them knew if or when another attempt at invasion would happen, since the bombing of Hitler's prized Berlin the Luftwaffe had attacked every major city relentlessly. The lads had done an amazing job fighting off the Luftwaffe once but who knew what Hitler had up his sleeve next? Now in the 3rd year of the war the air raids over the major towns and industrial sites had lessened, that was true, but every now and then there would be concentrated attacks on areas near the docks and ports, and just now there was another 'flare up' and their little town was on the receiving end. How poor Eliza felt she couldn't imagine her Thomas being in the Merchant Navy. Why? They all knew that the enemies' attention had turned to the seas and the Navy in an attempt to stop the supplies getting through.

They all knew of the mass burials that had taken place in the cities following the air raids, been told of the trains containing Jewish children pouring into the country, heaven knows what sights they had seen, the poor lambs. These were dangerous, wicked times. In her book Ruby was doing no harm, in fact, she thought of her as a ray of sunshine, someone who brought beauty into this wicked world with her joyful warmth and her laughter and music.

Ruby chattered brightly, animated as ever, retelling of the happenings of last evening when she had been biking along the dark lanes, hurrying home when the raid had started.

She laughingly explained how John Parker had clipped the front basket of her bike with his jeep and caused her to tumble off into a hedge and how following this she had stayed over at the base on a bed in the medical room.

Gazing at the American officer fondly she described a late night spent with John drinking Bourbon and talking into the early hours of the morning.

Frances listened carefully, detecting the intense energy between the two and the sparkling light in her friend's eyes when the American officer glanced over. He made no secret of the depth of his regard for her best friend and Frances wondered if Ruby had broken her golden rule of 'Never become too involved with a Yank, they will love you and leave you without a second glance and maybe leave you with a surprise present at that.'

Sitting just now she was reminded of her Joseph, of the way that he used to be with her, of his dark almost brooding passionate gaze, of his protectiveness, of his strength and tenderness, and all the familiar memories of their times together flooded her with such deep emotion that she suddenly felt overwhelmed and for one embarrassing moment she wondered if she was going to faint.

Rushing out of the kitchen in haste she leant on the cold scullery wall.

Lizzie was aware that Frances was 'On the edge' and decided to let her have 'a breather.'

Ruby chattered on, explaining that her bike had been repaired by a willing serviceman before it had been loaded onto the jeep and was now leaning on the front wall outside.

John Parker talked with a passion for his fine home in the Southern States of America, of the wide open spaces and the endless sky, where he would sit on the porch in the evening and watch the clouds racing across a turquoise sky until the sunset in a blaze of burning orange against the indigo heavens.

Ruby listened, completely romanced by John's description of his home, "Wow, it all sounds so beautiful."

He said with longing of his hard-working parents and of him being their eldest son, thanking providence that his younger brother had not passed the Army Medical and so they still had someone at home if he didn't return.

Ruby squeezed his hand, touched by the yearning and sadness in his voice she swallowed and rubbed her eyes.

"More tea love" Ruby enquired, jumping up quickly.

At that moment Frances wondered back in to join them, she had splashed her face with cold tap water and smoothed her crumpled blouse, aware that she was still wearing her heavy factory overalls.

"No thanks I'll pass on this one, I need to get back to the base" John answered with a tinge of regret.

"Safe journey then lad" Lizzie answered softly.

Frances hastily pushed her heavy black hair back from her face and smiled, shaking his hand.

The two women watched as Ruby followed John out onto the street.

"He's easy on the eye, that's without a doubt" Lizzie giggled.

Tall and lean with his dark hair cut in a crew cut, Lieutenant Parker certainly made for an imposing figure in his immaculately pressed, quality, American uniform.

Frances couldn't argue, he had a look of 'her Joseph,' only Joseph was broader on his shoulders and he had a wave to his hair.

Outside, John turned his collar up against the cold dampness of the early evening. Looking up at the pale unwelcoming greyness he thought of home and yearned for the homeliness and familiarity of all that he'd left behind. He knew that he was ready to settle down but the future loomed in front of him as uncertain and ominous. 'Who knew what mischief fate had in store for him?'

John climbed into the jeep and turned to hug Ruby.

"Penny for them John," Ruby laughed as she stared into the depths of his pale grey/blue eyes.

"For what?" he asked incredulously, pushing his cap off and scratching his head.

"It's something we say when we notice that someone is deep in thought, and you were 'away with the fairies,'" Ruby explained.

"I was away with what? He asked, incredulously. Oh! Never mind honey."

Yes, he'd been thinking of Ruby's friend Frances for a moment. She sure was a doll with that heavy coal black hair and the stunning deep emerald green eyes. But it was Ruby with her womanly wiles, his shapely Ruby with the dark liquid brown eyes that melted his heart. Ruby with her flaming red hair, was honest enough to share herself with him, she was all that he wanted and needed.

Last night she had sung for him, sung a soft Celtic melody that had captured his heart. She didn't have a spiteful, selfish bone in her body and respected her honesty and earthiness. They had both 'been around the block' but he knew that Ruby was not cheap or fickle and he knew that he could trust a woman who was so unusually open about her past and her needs.

John leant forward and held onto Ruby tightly.

"You do something to me Honey, you're all I want and need at this moment and for all the moments ahead. Sure I've messed around and had my share of wartime romance but I want you and me to come out of the war together."

Ruby shivered in the cold air, "Sweet talk Lieutenant."

"No! When all this is over I want you to be my wife." He whispered, gently tilting her chin upwards and kissing her hard on her mouth before he pulled back and reluctantly started the jeep up.

She listened as the engine trembled and shook and then sprung into life and pulled away.

She watched and waved until it disappeared in the distance and then turned and joined Frances and Lizzie in the kitchen.

Her heart was still thumping.

"So, this was real love, I've fallen in love at

last," She mused.

With a broad smile on her flushed face, she grabbed hold of Lizzie, pulled the roller out of Lizzie's wiry hair and danced her around the kitchen.

"You made quite an impression" she laughed.

"Ruby!" Frances protested, not wanting to embarrass their elderly friend

Both girls held a deep affection for Lizzie who was like a mother to them, but Ruby knew that Lizzie would be able to laugh her earlier performance off now that the American was no longer in their company.

"Oi, watch my old bones, my joints are creaking and crunching like old pipes, and my plumbing's not too brilliant either," Lizzie protested laughingly.

The clock struck on the hour, 5 pm, suddenly cutting into their momentary, jolly escape from the horrific reality of last night's raid.

On hearing the solemn chime Frances had withdrawn back into the heaviness once more. She sensed an ominous presence, something indefinable. They were all aware that they were 'living on a knife edge,' but this was something different, something that she couldn't identify, but it was there still, very real to her. She shuddered.

"Thank God you are safe Ruby, it was a bad night."

She broke the news to Ruby quietly.

"The factory is gone and Eliza has returned home with Sam whilst things are sorted out, she had a fright when the shelter took a blast. Jimmy managed to pull her out; she had fainted or been knocked unconscious. I was just off to work when Jimmy brought her back."

Ruby sighed, "She's not going to find it easy being under her father's roof again. Just because she's a married woman won't change the way he is, not while Thomas is away, he will see that it is his duty to keep her safe."

Lizzie interrupted sharply.

"Maybe it will do her good to get her priorities right and spend some time with those boys, too much time on her hands, it's not always healthy is it?."

"Eliza needs company," Lizzie continued angrily, "and while the factory is out of production she would soon get browned off."

Frances and Ruby were surprised at Lizzie's manner and looked on in surprise.

Lizzie explained hastily, "You know what some can be like, rumours, curtains twitching. Jimmy's been hanging around and Eliza misses her old man I know, but, do I have to put it into words? This war takes its toll on marriages, it'll do her good to be home for a while."

Frances had been stoking the fire. She stopped in her tracks, the truth suddenly dawning! That teacup! It had been Eliza's, of course.

She looked up at Lizzie whose glance back gave a warning. An unspoken 'Do not let on, we need to keep a lid on it' look.

Ruby reacted to Lizzie's stern seeming rebuke of Eliza.

"She's not heard news of Thomas for eight months Lizzie, nothing! Don't be too hard on her."

Lizzie sighed. "Nothing is clear-cut Ruby I

know that, but it's always the women who carry the can if anything goes too far, we all know that. Eliza is a dreamer, her Tom adores her, and he'd be broken when or if he got home and heard rumours. Sam, he will protect her, he's hot headed at times but he loves his daughter."

Ruby listened carefully, Lizzie's words of wisdom made sense, they all knew of others who had been left 'holding the baby, literally.'

Whereas this would never be the case for Ruby, she was worldly and made sure that this possibility would never happen. There were precautions that one could take, and despite her enjoying male company, having sex with them was not something that she ever promised, when she did it was a rare occasion.

Lizzie glanced over at Frances, noting her paleness and fidgeting. The last few days had been exhausting for all of them.

"You look done in Love; we'll be off and leave you in peace. I've got a couple of pig's trotters for our tea Ruby, besides which I need to sew these trousers, it's draughty."

They all chuckled.

CHAPTER 6.

Norma and her daughters were now back home after being treated at the church hall after the raid. The windows had been boarded up for the present and Harold and Violet had returned with them to sweep up the mess and make the place more cheerful for the girls. For now it suited them all.

Harold and Violet still needed to get back home to salvage and collect what was left of their belongings but the wreckage of their little house was still smouldering and it needed to be made safe.

Norma welcomed their company and another pair of hands, believing that their presence would comfort the girls. Besides, Harold and Violet needed a home and Reg would have wanted her to help,

"You are coming back with us" she'd insisted when Violet had worriedly stated, "You've enough to do as it is."

"There's nothing more to be said or done, you'd do the same for me, we can all 'muck in' together," said Norma warmly and she had kissed Violet on her cold cheek and welcomed them into her home. The girls were ecstatic to have the elderly couple's pet with them and were already vying for who should have him sleep on the end of the bed with them.

Harold and Violet both knew that they were very fortunate to be alive. Theirs had been a good marriage and despite the usual ups and downs, they had found that the hardships they'd experienced in the early years had only brought them closer together.

"What will the lads think?" worried Violet.

"We'll have to get word to them once we are sorted Vi, but for now try not to fret, we don't want to worry them just yet" answered Harold in a 'no-nonsense' manner.

Forever thankful for the Fire Wardens and Fire Fighters pulling them out from the heat and rubble of their home the couple still hadn't wanted to put on the good nature of Arthur and Joanie. After being given some basic first aid at the church hall Norma had invited them back to stay with her.

Reg was away fighting and the girls were a concern. The youngest, little Margaret had been sitting in the church hall with a blanket pulled over her head, refusing to be coaxed from underneath, even for a rare bit of toffee and a hug from her mum.

Harold had peeped underneath the blanket; wagging his finger teasingly he had promised a frightened Margaret a piggyback home. A shadow of concern had passed over Violet's face but Harold's brown eyes had twinkled and he had given his wife a reassuring smile.

Harold had promised the Vicar and those gathered about that there would be a treat of a bit of bacon once Arthur and himself had finished a little job that they had to see to. Then he had hauled a clinging Margaret onto his back and they had set off home.

Harold was more knocked about than he had

first realised but with a surge of adrenaline, he had raced the last few yards back to Norma's home. Violet had followed on, more slowly with a heavy tread. She was feeling her age and a troubling ache down her arm was niggling at her. Furtively she rubbed her arm, she didn't want any fuss.

Norma and Violet settled the girls with toast and pork dripping and cups of hot sweet tea and then had sent them into the front room to play with their dollies.

They were to be kept close at home whilst Norma considered how best she could keep them safe. Soon enough the sound of giggling and shouting escaped the front room, the children had an ability to bounce back and were mostly cheerful in the face of the daily happenings around them. At the moment they were not attending school because the building had been hit in an air raid and it hadn't been made safe for use. The oldest was particularly pleased that she was now spared the indignity of PE, having to jump around in navy knickers and vest in the hall was not to her liking.

Just for now they were back home, their bellies were full and mum and Harold and Violet, who they called Aunty and Uncle were all together in their house, and now they had dear Scoffer too. Reg and the older couple had been friends over many years and the girls felt safe with them being there. All was well in the girls' world for now.

Norma made her double bed up with clean linen and decided to let Harold and Violet have her front bedroom with the double bed. She would sleep with the two younger girls in the small back bedroom.

Whilst making sure that the elderly couple were comfy, each with an armchair in front of the stove, she felt suddenly weary, as if all her energy had 'just drained away.' Steadying herself she realised that she hadn't eaten anything for a good while and she had refused food offered from 'those kindly souls up at the church hall,' being too worried about her daughters at the time, of course.

"Well, I can soon put that right," she reasoned.

Harold and Violet were both dozing, their heads were slumped forward, and they both looked exhausted, poor things. Harold was snoring softly and murmuring in his sleep. Creeping around them she put a light under the corned beef stew and then cut herself a slice of bread and spread it with the last of the dripping, suddenly feeling ravenous.

Norma took herself upstairs to the back bedroom and sat heavily on the girls' bed. Quietly she whispered a prayer, thanking God for keeping them all safe, giving thanks for the roof still above their heads and asking that "Please God, keep my Reg safe wherever he may Be, Amen."

She stayed upstairs for a while, tidying and fussing and fretting.

"What would happen to them all if the worst did happen and if things continued to go the way that they were?" she fretted, more worried about her four young daughters than herself.

The thought of living in an occupied country under German oppression terrified her. Although the newsreels and the Servicemen's letters arriving back home were of necessity, heavily censored, they still heard horrifying stories from some of the evacuees from Europe, who had luckily made it to British shores, and were working and living alongside them. Trying to remain 'solid' for the girls, she had given up on reading the 'Daily's' because they were full of doom or gloom.

"Right" she scolded. She smoothed her hair and rubbed her face with a flannel and tidied her piny. For now, they had survived, they were together. They were with good friends and they would continue to battle on.

Rushing downstairs she called out to the girls, waking Violet with a jolt.

"So, everybody, let's get the ginger beer out, Susan get the glasses and we'll listen to a bit of music on the wireless."

The girls tumbled out of the front room; Harold woke with a snore and a start. And Violet smiled. "Lovely."

Night fell, it was still raining heavily, and Arthur and Joanie sat in comfortable silence, both working on a peg rug for their kitchen. Arthur was ready to turn in early tonight. Last night's raid had been full on and this evening he was not just weary but his heart was heavy. Arthur was always ready to do his bit but the visions of last night's carnage haunted him every time he closed his eyes. He had been a hero by night when the adrenaline was surging through his body, but the late morning when he'd managed to get home he soon felt every year of his age. Harold and Violet losing their home was bad enough but he tried to take comfort from the fact that at least they had both survived to see another day.

"Aye, another day of what?" he sighed.

Joanie leant forward. "Penny for them Arty" she smiled.

He gazed up into his wife's gentle face; she was still so very beautiful and dear to him. Impulsively he leant forward and kissed her cheek. Arthur was not one to reveal his innermost thoughts or be demonstrative; he'd never been comfortable with it. Joanie was delightedly surprised.

"Didn't realise I'd dropped off love, I'm not going to be much help to you on this rug I'm afraid" he apologised.

"I've been thinking of our boys Arty, I mean, I always do, but this time it's different, I can't seem to settle" Joanie fretted.

"Well it's only natural love, our boys are in the Air Force and watching the raid last night it's impossible not to wonder and worry about them. I suppose there is some comfort in James and Gordon being together. To think all over the world there are lads and lasses fighting for us, risking their lives every day. It's hard to bear but I'm proud of them both and we know it's in God's hands, there's nothing we can do about it."

"There's no other way than for us all to fight, we are struggling each day to survive and they are fighting for their lives each time their plane goes up in the sky to take on Hitler's Luftwaffe. Sixteen weeks the battle of Britain lasted, so many young lives lost, we owe them everything Joanie, and we'd have been invaded by the Buggers now if our lads hadn't succeeded. Those Nazis, well, they were too sure of themselves, they were too cocky. That narrow strip of water between us and France defeated them, unbelievable really! But I do wonder how much longer it will all go on for, with Denmark, Norway, Belgium, Luxembourg and France under their heel." Arthur finished his unusual tirade and leant over to reach for his pipe.

"No baccy," he moaned. He picked up the newspaper but threw it down on the chair in disgust, "Heaven knows, these rags are all censored and make for a depressing read, anyway, I don't think I'll bother. Thank God the Yanks joined us, that's all, aye, it's a broken world."

Joanie put the rug away and wandered over to the sideboard, looking sadly at the photographs of her sons. Rummaging in the top drawer she pulled out a small package and handed it to Arthur.

"Well, where did this come from?" Arthur's face lit up in surprise.

Joanie tipped her finger to the side of her nose cheekily, "Friends of Ruby," she laughed.

She watched as he scooped the baccy into his tin and then carefully filled the bowel of his pipe. They sat in silence as the pungent smoke drifted upwards towards the already yellow stain on the ceiling.

"He's a good man" Joanie mused.

Joanie's gaze once again took in the many photographs of her sons displayed in a proud array on the dark polished oak.

"My dreams are full of them;" she whispered. "Every day it gets more difficult to put on a cheery face, each blinking day it gets harder, who knows where any of this will end. I remember my mum's words, you know, what she used to say to me when I was a girl and feeling a bit low. "The sun will burst through when you least expect it!" She was right then, it always did in those days" Joanie mused.

"Shush" Arthur hastily interrupted.

They both listened to the tread of heavy footsteps on the gravel outside as they became louder and louder and watched as the door slowly opened. James filled the doorway, looking handsome and incredibly smart in his RAF uniform.

"James," Joanie cried rushing forward. "Where's Gordon?"

James was slow to respond. "He's recovering mum, he will be okay."

"I knew it, now it all makes sense" Joanie cried."

"I should have written but I know that you don't always get our letters, and it seemed better to wait and tell you face to face on my next leave. Sit down both of you and I can explain, he's in the hospital and he's got a few burns but the Doctors say he's going to be fine. Look mum, he's being well cared for." James added hastily.

James had dreaded telling his parents, his mum in particular, she idolised her boys, always had. He'd known that this would be difficult and he looked to Arthur for help.

"Come on now Joanie, give the lad a chance to sit down and then he can tell us properly, why don't you put the kettle on," Arthur said calmly, feeling anything but! James had related as much as he could, and then remembered his promise to his brother Gordon.

James knocked quietly on Frances's door and she stared for a moment, and then laughingly invited him inside. They sat huddled together listening to the wireless. After breaking the news of his brother's crash landing to his parents and reassuring them that the only injuries that Gordon had sustained were burns to his hands, he had needed to get away from his mum's questioning and distress. He simply didn't have the emotional resources at the moment; he was barely holding himself together. He had rushed out to get some air and a cigarette. The Blackout meant that he couldn't light up outside and besides, it was bitingly cold so he'd decided to pay a visit to Frances and keep his promise to Gordon.

Frances took the news calmly, quietly noting the strain around James eyes and his pallor. He explained that Gordon's burns had initially been slow to respond to treatment but the medics had started a new regime and at last the skin was healing. It was believed that Gordon would have full use of his hands with some help from physiotherapy and when James had left his brother in the hospital he had been enjoying the attention from some very pretty nurses.

Frances thought back in time to when Gordon had held a torch for her and the problems that it had caused because he'd never tried to hide it. This had provoked considerable friction between Gordon and Joseph. On Frances's part, she had never encouraged Gordon but she had genuinely valued his friendship. Gordon was one of those men that were comfortable sharing and talking about his emotions and in Frances's world, this was rare. Gordon had taught Frances to play chess and Joseph had resented the time that they had spent together.

When Joseph had watched them with their heads close together over the chessboard he had wanted to haul Gordon across the board and throw him out. It had been a question of Joseph's jealous possessiveness against Gordon's stubbornness, with neither men meeting in the middle. The outcome was not surprising! Stalemate! Finally, Frances had asked Gordon not to visit because the tension that used to build up between herself and Joseph would often result in fireworks.

Joseph's love for Frances was passionate and his jealousy hurt like hell, emotionally and physically, right in the pit of his stomach. He would try to reason it out and control his temper but he was unable to do so, or explain it either. It had come to the point that the mere sight of Gordon's sandy hair and moustache and heavy build would set his teeth on edge. Frances had finally stepped in, time with Joseph had become precious, he was her world too, and with war looming she had acted decisively. Gordon had accepted her wishes and backed off, there were no hard feelings.

James was a 'different kettle of fish' and she was pleased to share his company this evening, with winter closing in the long dark nights seemed to grow ever longer and they listened quietly to the wireless playing soft tunes sharing a cigarette. James, normally the joker of the two brothers was lost in his own world of aircraft and fires and friends not returning. He was relieved that his brother had not been trapped when his plane had crash landed and thankful that he'd been dragged out before it exploded in flames.

Before coming home on leave Gordon had been laughing and joking with the nurses and although he wasn't completely sure how badly disabled his hands would be he was managing to remain hopeful. He had asked his brother to pop in and check to see how Frances was coping and James was happy to do so.

So here he was sitting in the kitchen listening to Vera Linn, but none of this felt real. His world and family were back on the base. He had become accustomed to a different reality, an impermanence where every minute he felt alive, exhilarated, followed by exhaustion and fear and loss, empty beds and new faces.

James had become adjusted to veering from mission to mission, to the alcohol-fuelled jokes and singsongs and piano playing and camaraderie. He was often exhausted but still found it difficult to sleep and when he did the nightmares would kick in or he would be woken by one of the others screaming or sobbing in their own private world of torment.

Realistically he didn't hold out any hope of dying of old age in his own bed, he didn't hope for much other than to go quickly and 'please God not to be shot and come down over the ocean.' He had an irrational fear of this happening and he would often dream of coming down into the freezing cold waves in the darkness, with blackness all around him, of shouting and shouting for help which never came, of the terrifying emptiness and loneliness which would stay with him on waking.

Frances glanced over at James sitting by her side, she noticed the tremor of his hands and she jumped up, coming back with a tot of sherry that she'd been keeping for what? "Better days?" She asked herself. Well, maybe they would be a long time coming. While he drank she told him of the loss of the engineering factory two nights before, of Eliza's lucky escape from the shelter with the help of Jimmy. She explained that Eliza was now home on the farm with Sam and Kathleen and the boys for now. She told him that she was at a loss really, just waiting for news of the factory starting up again and that she knew Jimmy would call in when he had any news.

James smiled, "It will be good to catch up with Jimmy, we used to have some good nights down at the Swan, it's a wonder we didn't get thrown out, Jimmy was always getting into hot water over one female or another."

Yes, Jimmy had been one of the lucky ones. He had been exempted from military service when his medical had established that he was fully colour blind. Jimmy didn't think so; he had been appalled and not a little humiliated. He had challenged the medics and demanded that the decision be overridden, with little effect. So, he'd laughed it off and hidden his disappointment in his usual way, "Wenching," as his Uncle Patrick called it, and gambling, cards, a game of Poker usually.

Being in a reserved occupation Jimmy worked locally at the nearby engineering factory and he had found it convenient to move in with his aunt Lil and uncle Patrick who lived two streets away from Frances. He was a popular cheeky lad and the girls found him attractive with his short brown curly hair and grey-green eyes which were always full of mischief and laughter. He was always a popular guest at any house party with his jokes and his banjo.

Jimmy's aunt, Lil had laughed and teased him, "Now I understood your awful choice of shirts and ties," but she was secretly very relieved and happy to have Jimmy still at home with them.

Jimmy didn't hide the fact that he loved female company, he didn't take offence at his uncle's jibes, it wasn't in his nature. But he'd never settled in a long-term relationship, although he liked to joke that he'd "had a few misses." Jimmy's work as a skilled toolmaker and engineer was vital in wartime and at this point in time, he was fully engaged in helping to set up the machinery to re-establish the new factory.

"Yes," James thought back to past escapades when he and Jimmy had been full of the enthusiasm and confidence of youth. He pictured Jimmy as a lad, scrawny and cheeky always with a wide smile and a ready laugh. "I'll pop round."

"How long a leave have they given you James?" Frances inquired.

"I've got four days left. The odd thing is now I've got time I can't settle, don't know what to do with myself, I just feel so bloody restless." James answered pushing his hair back.

"There's not much settling around here, we've had raids most nights, Norma's taken Harold and Violet in, Eliza's back home, there's been no news lately from Eliza's Thomas and Ruby is still back and forward to the AAS base. Lizzie's still pottering about and all of this time I can't get rid of the feeling that my Joe is still alive. Is it possible James? After all this time" Frances implored. "Sometimes I think I hear him calling me" she whispered. "And now Gordon's hands! God help him James" she cried.

James gave Frances a hard stare and suddenly leapt to his feet. He just couldn't cope with this. He had survived this last year by remaining detached for most of the time. He didn't have answers and didn't know how to comfort the fragile female sitting in front of him. He'd escaped his mother's crying, it had all been too overwhelming. He needed to 'cut and run,' have a couple of gins, maybe a game of darts, any distraction which would stop this sickening tide of emotions overflowing from deep inside of him.

James had dodged the emptiness that was with him the minute he opened his eyes and the fear that threatened to engulf him, by either avoiding company or by totally surrounding himself in the thick of it.

"I'm off to see Jimmy, catch you later" he cried and hugging Frances he bolted out of the door.

Lil opened the door. A tall figure in uniform loomed above her.

"James! Come in quickly, don't want to show any light or I'll have them wardens after me, or worse still the Luftwaffe. Well, you're a sight for sore eyes. It's a tonic to see you, you handsome brute. I was feeling a bit low just now, what a lovely surprise," Lil gushed.

James gave Lil a hasty hug asking her, "Is your Jimmy at home then?"

"Jimmy! Lil shouted up the stairs, "Come and see who's standing here in our kitchen."

Jimmy thundered down the stairs.

"James, blimey, good to see you mate, is your Gordon home?"

James quietly explained that his brother was injured and being treated for burns to his hands following a crash landing.

"Sorry to hear that son," Patrick sympathised

as he shook James's hand. Noticing the lad's pallor he quickly sat him down.

The two friends sat at the kitchen table. In the corner Patrick murmured occasionally, he was slumped in a half sleep state, exhausted after his duties with Arthur over the last few nights. The wireless was playing low and Lil was busy unpicking an old woolly of Jimmy's to re-knit into some warm socks for the war effort.

Sensing the tension in James, Jimmy got out a deck of cards.

"Let's have a bit of a game of Rummy and a drop of Aunt Lil's Rhubarb wine" he suggested glancing quickly at Aunt Lil with a silent request for help. Lil hastily bustled over to her sideboard and proudly produced a bottle and four glasses.

"Something smells nice Aunty Lil" Jimmy hinted.

"It's just pig chitterlings lads, it's the only meat I could get this time, Butcher was running a bit short, Lizzie had the last two pigs trotters. Still, they should be nice, I've simmered them with a nice onion and a couple of potatoes for a good few hours. Like some?" She offered warmly.

The three men all nodded their approval.

"Here you are then lads, tuck in" and she placed two steaming bowls in front of them and took Patrick's over to him on a tray. This was plain wartime food but James ate slowly, savouring each tasty mouthful. He hadn't realised how hungry he was.

"Be good to have a get-together before your leave is up James. I'll be back on shifts again soon, the factory should be up and running again in a week or two. I've been helping out this morning, in fact, now that we've found another location, didn't take long for those in the know to find us some more machinery either." Jimmy chatted eagerly, tailing off when he suddenly took in the haunted expression on his mate's face,

Staring back at him James' eyes were pools of darkness without a glimmer of light.

Jimmy shuddered, something was wrong, he was uneasy and fearful for his friend's sanity, he'd heard of other's 'losing their marbles.' Not sure what to do he leant forward and squeezed his friends arm supportively.

James stared hard in front of him and suddenly with a jolt he smiled and apologised.

"Sorry mate, I'm just a bit tired you know. So, Eliza had a lucky escape then Jim, glad that you were around to pull her free," James smiled craftily.

Jimmy frowned, sighing heavily. "It was bad James. It was hell finding our way out through the smoke and debris. I think it was Eliza's perfume that half led me to her. She's back with the twins on the farm for now. I can't see Sam being agreeable to letting her come back, to be honest with you. But, she wants to 'do her bit,' she's not one to duck her responsibilities. Besides, she knows the kids are safer where they are and their grandma Kathleen adores them."

James nodded, "Any news of Tom?"

"No, there's not been a dickybird for the last eight months. She's finding it hard, not knowing if or what's happened. We all know the dangers he faces, it's a risky business." Jimmy considered.

"Used to hold a torch for Eliza Jimmy?"

James whispered.

"Yes, I did and still do, I can't deny it, can't help myself, but she's married to Thomas and has those two little ones. Usually, I see her on shift at the factory. We're good mates but nothing more can come of it. Although if the worst happened I'd be happy to take her and the boys on," Jimmy answered softly, whilst turning slightly to check whether his Uncle Patrick was listening.

Patrick leant forward, he was listening!

"I've told you Jimmy, Sam would never stand for any of your messing about with his daughter. Give her a wide berth, she's a pretty little thing but she has a man away at sea," scolded Patrick. He'd no patience for Jimmy's chancy behaviour with females and it sometimes infuriated him how Lil always managed to find excuses for him. "It's about time you grew up my lad" he admonished, wagging his finger.

Grudgingly Jimmy agreed, he wasn't one to take umbrage. "I know Uncle Patrick, I've told you, and I'll stay away."

But secretly he knew that Eliza was the woman that he adored, the only one that had captured his heart. He wanted to protect her, to romance her, dress her in silk and black lace. He dreamt of holding her and he didn't have too much guilt about Eliza's Thomas. He knew what they got up to in the merchant navy, Tom was no innocent, he thought defiantly.

"Is there anyone for you James?" asked Lil, hastily trying to take the heat out of the situation.

"No one will have me Lil" James winked at Jimmy cheekily.

Patrick laughed, feeling embarrassed now at his testiness with his nephew, he offered James a cigarette and they all sat quietly together, listening to the wireless playing low and to the mournful sound of the wind moaning and shrieking down the chimney.

Jimmy was lost in his thoughts of Eliza, of the way her hair turned to the colour of ripening barley in the autumn, of long ago when he had helped out at the farm. When he had thought that he stood a chance! Back to the afternoons when they had lay on their stomachs amongst the buttercup grass, feeling the heat of the sun on their backs, and he had stolen the first kiss.

Sam had sniffed around suspiciously, ever watchful and creeping up on them he had startled them shouting, "Right lad, I'll soon put a stop to that!" They had been innocent fourteen-year-olds and Jimmy had meant no harm, but Sam had stopped him helping out. Eliza had become isolated and resentful and Jimmy had moved on.

"Would you listen to that?" Patrick inquired of himself as the wind rose and blew its' forceful way through the attic, rattling and shaking windows. Lil hastily checked that the blackout curtains were tightly closed.

James took this movement as the opportunity to leave; he kissed Lil on the cheek and left quietly by the back door.

CHAPTER 7.

For the next two days, the weather was cold and damp and the clouds hung low and heavy in the grey mauve sky. The dull weather and thick cloud brought some respite from the raids, partly because of the poor visibility.

After sifting through the ruins of their little home Harold and Violet were making themselves comfortable and useful at Norma's. Scoffer was in his element, the girls pandered to his every whim and when he felt that he wasn't getting enough attention he just had to 'donk' them with his big, soft paws and they would rush to find his brush, or even better find him a titbit. Yes, he was in 'Doggy heaven,' that was for sure!

Norma had now received two letters from Reg which she had read and re-read.

"My dear little pumpkin" they had started. Norma knew that she was plain, but her husband had never seen her in that light, he adored her, and she adored him. She had guarded his words jealously, only showing the last few lines to the girls which their father had put in especially for them. Despite their initial excitement when the letters had arrived the girls were fretful, it seemed that the news from their father had unsettled them rather than giving comfort.

Harold and Violet brought some warmth and security to the home and Violet welcomed the business of family life again, although she noticed that she had lost a lot of her strength lately. She dismissed it and put it down to the shock of losing her home, and old age.

"I'm no spring chicken anymore" she would laugh when Harold became concerned.

Harold insisted on making trips to the allotment where he would slowly and painfully try to salvage anything that had survived. Although there was little growing at this time of year he had stored the potatoes and apples and onions that had been harvested in September and October and he made a few journeys back and forth with these.

Violet had pickled the beetroot and cucumber and made some lovely chutney with the green tomatoes, she'd made a couple of jars of blackberry jam too but she had been worried that it wouldn't keep too well because she had been low on sugar. This would have seen them through the winter, but now all of her lovely produce had gone, along with their house.

Miraculously two of the hens and the Cockerel had survived and Harold had quickly rounded them up with the help of the girls, happy that there were still three bags of the grain rations that were still forthcoming from the Government. The hens now clucked away happily although the Cockerel was prone to be temperamental, and if you caught him in the wrong mood he would make a swift charge at your shins in spite. Even Scoffer was very wary of him following a surprised morning attack. Each afternoon there were fun and laughter as they were encouraged or chased into the air raid shelter at night.

Although there were constant fear and disruption these wartime days soon became a normal reality, waking each day to people in the streets focused on survival and daily routine. Some managed better than others that were true; some 'went completely off the rails.'

"The strangest circumstances eventually become 'the norm,'" Violet would state to herself when she would hear about some of the 'goings on' in the street.

Violet had written to both of her sons warning them of the loss of their home, carefully reassuring them both that she and Harold, and Scoffer, were safe, and staying with Norma and the girls for the time being. She knew that there was no sure way of knowing if or when they would receive her news because she guessed they were overseas with their regiment, but she remained hopeful.

"Well, you have to be these days, don't you" she softly mumbled to herself as she licked and sealed the envelopes.

Letters had arrived sporadically from both of their sons and Violet felt 'sure in her bones' that they were still alive.

The elderly couple remained mostly stoic, accepting their fate with cheerful resolve to 'make the best of it' and soldier on.

"There are lots worse off than us Violet," Harold would firmly declare when he recognised Violet was wavering and a bit fretful.

"It's alright for you" she mumbled, "You come back from the pub with Arthur half pickled."

Harold peered into his wife's face smiling kindly, realising that his wife had taken the loss of her home and womanly treasures much harder than himself. He'd noticed fragility about her the last day or two. He smoothed Violet's loosely gathered grey hair with his rough hands, marvelling at its luxuriant thickness even still in her old age.

"Why don't you and the other ladies have a get-together at Lizzie's," he suggested, "a good old 'rabbiting' session with the girls will do you the world of good. You can come back and tell me what's in store for us in that Crystal Ball of hers."

Violet paused, looking into Harold's smiling eyes she hugged him tightly, then grabbing her thick brown cardigan she wrapped it around her shoulders.

"I'm always cold lately"

Harold tapped her on her ample bottom, giving her a crooked smile, eyes twinkling.

"I can warm you up, old girl."

"Cheeky! I'm off to Lizzie's," she called as she rushed down the passage.

Frances and Lizzie were sitting companionably, warming themselves near the stove, waiting for the pot of tea to brew. The rain beat loudly on the windows and the street was flooding during the heavy downpour which had been threatening for the last three days. The crying sound of the storm filled Frances with dread. She had existed in a state of fluctuating hope, insecurity and apprehension for weeks now and lately she had relied heavily on Lizzie's wisdom and their strong connection to give her some sort of balance.

Too often she would wake up suddenly in the dark, finding herself trembling and confused. The dreams of being with Joseph were vivid, his physical presence and the sensation of his embrace would flood her whole body with such a joy followed by a crushing disappointment when she woke with a start, in a sweat to a cold, bitter bedroom.

Frances was a believer of the existence of the human soul after death, and she found comfort in her belief that if Joseph was dead then they would meet up again someday, in fact, it was this firm belief that helped her to get through. But the past two weeks she had felt as if Joe was haunting her, trying to get back to her, trying to connect, and she didn't know how to help him.

Lizzie offered sanctuary and visions of the future, along with her logical approach and advice that at some point Frances would be able to move forward with her life. Frances found that just sitting in Lizzie's kitchen 'grounded' her, helped her find peace somehow. Lizzie always provided a warm loving welcome and her home did the same. Lizzie kept it sparkling clean with her bicarbonate soda and vinegar, with the dried lavender and lemon balm sewn into handkerchiefs made into little parcels, with 'a bit of green' and a few berries in the winter.

"You don't need riches to do this, you can create your very own loving welcome and fill your home with light Frances" Lizzie would advise. "I haven't had a lot to spare being a widow these last years but I've always found comfort in Mother Nature. A few rose petals and a bottle of Glycerine from the herbalist does wonders for your complexion and the rainwater from the water butt keeps your hair lovely and soft. Sing a song and scrub the floor and keep love in your heart, it will get you through.

Frances tried! But meanwhile, she missed the

daily routine of work and wondered when Jimmy would bring news that the factory had been set up so that she could rejoin the welcome distraction of routine and production.

For now she listened to the wireless, listened for the sirens, listened to a delighted Ruby declaring her love for John Parker, and waited for news or a visit from Eliza.

Lizzie noted the darkening shadows under Frances's eyes and was aware of her young friend's increasing remoteness. She bustled into the room and plonked herself down heavily, inviting Frances to join her.

"Right then chick, the tea is brewed, I'll pour out and afterwards we'll have a little gaze into my Crystal."

The pot of tea was drained, the cups were cleared away and she slowly unwrapped the soft purple cloth and gently placed the globe in front of her. Usually, Frances would have attempted to read the tea leaves but after finishing the pot of weak tea the usual keenness to try had not materialised.

"Sit down in front of me pet." Lizzie invited.

Frances could feel her heart thumping rapidly in her breast, with a wave of nausea sweeping over her; she wondered if she should be asking this of Lizzie today, she was 'neither here nor there.'

"Take some deep breaths love, slowly, now, is that better?"

Frances felt the tears welling up in her eyes. Taking slow deep breaths for a few moments she was able to calm the rising panic which had threatened to engulf her.

"Maybe a little chat first," Lizzie soothed.

"I'm a mess Lizzie," Frances whispered. "All of this time I've coped. I've managed and existed without Joseph. Now I'm having these vivid dreams of us being together and sometimes when I'm awake I hear him calling me, his presence is so strong that I expect to turn around and see him standing there. I Just need to know Lizzie, where is he now? What's he doing?" Frances looked up at Lizzie intently.

Lizzie held Frances's hands tenderly and guided her.

"When love has a strong bond then it draws us together and it continues after we've passed. When you think of him or speak to him Frances then he will know. If he is in spirit, or still alive somewhere, then in his quiet moments he will feel your presence, as you do his."

Frances nodded.

"Please carry on Lizzie, don't hold back, I need to know."

Gazing into the crystal ball Lizzie waited for the cloudiness to clear. Lizzie's mystical powers and inner knowing had been second nature to her since she was a young child; in fact, she had thought as a child that her experiences were completely normal and natural to all. Until she had experienced the reactions of others when she had shared her insights and the happenings that were common to her as she grew up.

The elderly widow focused on the picture that was appearing in front of her. She peered into the mist and as it cleared a tall figure strolled towards her, walking unsteadily. She saw a man in uniform, waving both arms, throwing his cap into the air. There was a Red Cross ambulance and he turned and waved at the vehicle as it sped away into the distance. The sun burst through and a faint hint of pink lit up the sky. The tall figure smiled, he was holding a bouquet of lush, deep red roses and he blew a kiss. Then the vision faded and the crystal was once again clear.

Lizzie was aware of Frances's scrutiny.

"Lizzie, please, tell me, what do you see, I want the truth now, for good or bad" Frances rushed her words.

Lizzie smiled, she beamed, relieved that she did not have to be cautious or sparing with the telling.

"He's coming home, your Joseph is coming home, he's on his bloody way home," she laughed. "He's injured but he's okay, he's coming home at last!"

The two women held each other tightly, laughing and crying tears of joy, dancing and jigging around the kitchen not noticing Violet who was standing in the doorway.

"Good news then?" she laughed and joined in with the hugs and happiness.

Midnight had been slumbering in the corner by the stove and woken by the hubbub. He protested, meowing loudly he shot forward and collided into the three women dancing around in joyous abandonment, two of them happy with the good news and the third just joining in to chase away the bleakness and the sameness of her days.

Midnight knew that his master was returning, he felt it too and wondered what all of the commotion was about.

Females, he thought, it will be good to have my friend Joseph back and some male company in the house.

Jumping up onto the table he knocked over the milk jug and unnoticed he lapped up the creamy spillage, luxuriantly licking away the white froth from his whiskers. Unnoticed he stretched out on the velvety chenille material and pulled his claws down the length of Lizzie's beautiful chestnut brown tablecloth before finally slinking back through the back door.

Suddenly Violet plonked down with a loud 'Oomph.'

"Crikey, sorry ladies, I'm feeling a bit dizzy, feeling my age these days" she laughed in embarrassment.

Frances and Lizzie paused, looking carefully at Violet Lizzie pulled her spectacles back in place and she noticed her friend fidgeting with the sleeve of her cardigan. There was an uneasy pause before Lizzie gently stepped forward and leaning towards Violet gently reassured her.

"All of this upset and change has taken it out of you that's all, you'll soon be as right as rain. Are you doing too much at Norma's Violet? The girls are lovely but they can be a handful. I'm sure that it will all come right in the end and the lads and your Harold will sort something out."

The last thing that Violet wanted was to bring the mood down. She had an inner knowing that something had changed for the worse since Arthur had pulled her and Harold from the ruins of their home. She just couldn't shake off this heaviness in her legs and the constant niggle in her arm that was causing considerable discomfort. Violet recognised that she was too long in the tooth to kid herself and she had strong suspicions that her ticker was damaged or simply worn out.

Violet did not fear on her own account but worried how Harold and the boys would take it if anything happened to her. She hated making a fuss or being the centre of attention and she planned to carry on quietly and 'keep mum.'

Violet missed her home; she had found some comfort there. When she was missing her boys badly she would take their clothes from the wardrobe and carefully iron their shirts and jackets, before gently folding and putting them away again. Harold would watch and sigh as she pressed the soft wool against her face and breathed it in. She couldn't do that now; all of their clothes and letters had gone, along with the ruins of her home. She longed to hear from them again, always waiting; her mother's intuition told her that they were still alive. She prayed each day for their safe return and put her trust in the Lord.

Knowing that Lizzie would pick up on her low energy Violet thought quickly so as not to alarm her. Grinning she excused herself saying.

"Oh you know what it can be like Lizzie, I'm just used to my own bed, although Norma has been very generous and has given us her and Reginald's bed. What with Harold's snoring and these raids I'm just a bit tired that's all. Anyway, I've come round to suggest a get-together for us women, thought we could all do with a bit of cheering up, what do you think?" Violet gushed, bustling around to avoid her friends' scrutiny.

Lizzie nodded her head in agreement.

"Ere, what's happened to your best cloth?" Violet exclaimed in horror.

Frances reddened and she jumped up guiltily, guessing the culprit.

"I can guess," Lizzie stated. She recognised Violet's hasty dismissal of her questioning and chose to let the matter drop for now, realising that now was not the time to push her concerns. The respect and responsibility that she held for her gift and her integrity in working with spirit were second nature to her after all of this time, so she tactfully retreated.

"Right, leave it to me then" Frances eagerly offered, "I'll need to act quickly before the factory is up and running. We'll catch Ruby tonight and pop around Joanie's now, maybe Jimmy or James could get word to Eliza. Is Saturday night alright with you Lizzie?

"Yes ducks," she answered, "You tell Norma then if you will please, Violet. I don't suppose Kathleen will join us knowing how her Sam views are, but you never know. Norma might bring us some of her bread pudding if you ask nicely."

Frances leant forward and kissed Lizzie on her whiskery cheek, noting that she smelt nicely of the Glycerine and Rosewater that she was fond of using.

"I'm off then," Frances replied, hugging Violet she quickly left, on a mission to find Midnight. She doubted whether he would show any evidence of his deeds this afternoon but she was going to check his claws anyway.

Violet hastily hitched up her wrinkled stockings over her swollen legs, apologising, "These blinking garters have had their day. Right, I'll leave you in peace Lizzie, I'll ask Lil too" she shouted as she followed Frances out.

In Ruby's bedroom, the draught from the wind forced its way through the narrow gaps between the leading and the glass and whispered a high-pitched, keening cry, waking Ruby with a start. She sighed, stretched and turned, then reached over to pull open the blackout curtains and look out onto the street. Yawning she looked up to the sky, and on seeing another cold grey morning she decided to climb back into her bed.

Ruby lay awake, her eyes wide open she stared up at the damp patch above her on the ceiling. Lizzie had been in a talkative mood last night and when the Luftwaffe planes flew over she'd resignedly joined her friend under the stairs. Sighing she turned to stare out of the window as the watery sun tried to make an appearance behind the heavy cloud.

Ruby was aware of the recent heavy losses of the American pilots during their daylight raids, and only yesterday she had witnessed an American Fighter touchdown and scrape in on its belly before bursting into flames. This time the fire had been successfully doused and the young crew had all managed to climb or be dragged out. The crew had quickly turned off the engine and so the flames were quickly dealt with without explosion.

The American Air Force had stepped up daylight bombing in an attempt to knock out the German war machine factories. John Parker told Ruby of how they would fly together in tight formation, of terrifying journeys in freezing temperatures, of the crew's superstitions and mascots and rituals that they practiced, in a desperate attempt to stay alive. They knew that they were lucky to have such well-equipped planes, trained pilots, good navigators and keen gunners, and efficient ground support. They all knew that their missions were absolutely essential; they believed that they had right on their side and the closeness between the crews sustained them. Grounded, John missed being part of all this.

Ruby accepted that her work at the base was a major part of her life now, along with the snatched moments with John Parker. Last night the enemy bombing has started around 7 pm and Ruby, although glad to be home with Lizzie had been so tired from the last two days spent at the base she'd felt as if she were listening to Lizzie from behind a pane of glass, far away, somehow.

She'd left the base well before the raid had started, without having a moment for a quick word or the usual embrace with John. Fortunately, she had reached home before the sirens called out and the bombing had started.

They had crept out from under the stairs in the very early hours and Ruby had climbed gratefully into her cold bed. She had lay there listening to Lizzie pottering down in the kitchen before falling into a fretful and restless sleep.

Now she was awake again, pondering how John had swept her off her feet with his passion and declarations of love and solemn promises that he wanted to spend the rest of his life with her, and take care of her, forever.

Ruby was aware of the seeming folly of falling for a 'yank,' attractive and handsome in their quality uniforms with their sweet talk and their promises and their very sexy American drawl. She was going into this with her eyes wide open and enjoying every lush moment of it.

Back on Sam and Kathleen's small farm Eliza dressed quickly and quietly, the working day began in the very early hours. The Grandfather clock which stood at the bottom of the stairs chimed solemnly, 4 am. The boys were cuddled closely together, only tufts of blonde hair showed above the tumble of blankets.

Sam was already up and out in the shed with the livestock, whilst Kathleen was bustling around the range cooker. The kettle was wobbling; just building up to steam and whistle, and a large saucepan of creamy porridge was already prepared and ready for any with a good appetite. The two helping hands would arrive at 5 am, but until then things were relatively quiet. The wireless played, fading in and out in the background, Sam liked to tune into the BBC news broadcast later on in the morning when he'd 'broke the back' of his duties but for now it was largely ignored, just providing a bit of background company for Kathleen, who for some reason felt uneasy, the usual peaceful quietness seemed oppressive somehow.

Eliza's thoughts were anything but quiet, the signs were unmistakable now. Initially, she'd brushed off the nausea and tiredness. When her 'monthly's' had been late she had dismissed their absence, telling herself that it was merely the long hours that she was covering at the factory and her snatched meals that were behind it all. For the last two days, her breasts had been tingly and sore and she knew with sinking recognition that this couldn't be anything else but pregnancy. Her exact fears were confirmed! She had been caught out, careless!

Eliza tried to calm herself; she remembered the last time that she and Thomas had been together, the fire in his eyes. Her feelings for him were so strong that they rushed out of the floodgate from her heart and she started to cry. She cried for another child to be brought into this uncertainty and war, she cried because she was frightened, she cried because she so wanted Tom to be beside her.

Kathleen spluttered on her tea and rushed towards her daughter.

"Whatever is the matter love?"

"Mum, I've been so stupid" Eliza sobbed.

Kathleen gently took hold of her daughter's shoulders.

"Lord, Oh I really hope you're not telling me what I think you're telling me" she gasped.

Eliza stared into her mother's face.

"That's the thing mum, I am, I'm carrying again."

Sam burst in bringing damp cold air into the warmth of the kitchen.

Sensing the tension he asked, "Eliza, why the tears?"

Noticing Kath's nervous smile her turned towards his wife and whispered in her ear.

"Is she a bit under the weather?"

Kathleen sighed, "Aye, something like that."

"I wonder, when this is all over if we'll ever return to the days before the war when a woman's work was to stay at home and raise the kids and look after our old man." she pondered.

Sam tactfully retreated, he stood over the sink, washing and splashing himself with cold water. Turning quickly, his face reddened from cold he advised,

"I think that 'do' at the factory has taken it out of you, maybe a night at Lizzie's will do you both good, but none of that 'He be je be' mind you!" he cautioned.

CHAPTER 8.

Saturday arrived, it was 6 pm and nearly the end of the week, a week in which there had been four heavy air raids, some in the street had received the dreaded news that loved ones had been injured, and worse, others had lost their homes, some had at long last received heart-warming letters from overseas, others such as Ruby had found romance, Eliza? The certainty that she was carrying a new life!

Lizzie's front parlour was inviting and comforting, the kitchen was warm and the table was laden with contributions of plain wartime food from the guests, Lil's homemade wine was especially welcome. Frances had brought her Victoria china tea set with the delicate violet patterns and gold rims, and all was set on a pure white linen tablecloth.

Lizzie, Ruby, Frances, Eliza, Kathleen, Norma and Joanie, Violet and Lil sat together in a tight circle in the now cramped front room. The tall fringed, standard lamp in the corner gave out a soft light and cast shadows across their faces. There was an air of quiet expectancy which was almost palpable.

In the kitchen, the men were playing card games. James, Jimmy, Patrick, Arthur, Harold and the American John Parker were quietly engrossed.

Norma's girls were staying with their Aunt, Gladys, who didn't have any children of her own and who according to Norma "Would spoil them rotten" for the weekend.

Sam had brought his family over to Lizzie's on the motorbike, squashing the excited twins and their gran in the sidecar whilst Eliza had ridden pillion. He'd made a hasty retreat from the gathering, "it really wasn't his cup of tea" and had ridden back home with the twins, arranging to collect his womenfolk at 10 pm. The boys would be in their beds then and he had asked a favour of Jean, a wife of one of his farm hands to 'pop in' and keep a check on them until they all returned. Sam wasn't sure what was going on exactly but after the other morning he was sure that 'something was afoot.'

The men had cleared a space at one end of a very full table and they were playing a game of cribbage. John Parker, intent on mastering a new game and the unique scoring system of pegging felt the anxiety and tension finally lessening. The Brits had made him feel at home and he received their friendly, good-natured teasing about Yanks with good grace.

John stretched his long uniformed legs out in front of him. Every now and then giggles erupted from the front room. It seemed to him the 'The Brits sure were resilient people, although their taste for cold mutton and Brussels sprouts left him cold.' He paused scratching his head, thinking over the events of the week and his declaration of love for Ruby. He was aware that there would be hurdles to pass before he and Ruby could finally be a married couple but he strongly believed that they could make their relationship work well. He knew in his heart that they were meant to be together and that when the war was finally at an end he would be able to persuade his girl of the wonderful opportunities they would be able to share back home in America. John was homesick, painfully so, for the wide open spaces and his younger brothers companionship.

Harold broke into John's thoughts "Come on John we can't wait all night, it's your turn lad," he teased. "The women will be out here soon and you'll still be pondering your next move at this rate."

The game carried on whilst the wireless played low and every now and then Jimmy would top up their glasses with a 'bit of the hard stuff' that John had brought over from the base.

"This is a real treat John, but I shan't have another or I'll be sloshed and I don't think my Joanie would be too happy if she was saddled with both me and James getting pickled," Arthur smiled. "The last time that I had a few too many I came home and ate all of our cheese rations for the week, she was vexed, to say the least. I'd tried to blame Frances's cat but my story didn't hold water."

"Well, we've a good table laid out tonight, thanks to the womenfolk pulling together," Harold cheerfully proclaimed as he reached furtively for the Bourbon.

Suddenly the front room door flung open and Jimmy watched as Eliza sidled past the table on her way to the 'lavvy.' James, already on the alert for any signs of indiscretion between the two warily glanced over at the pair. Eliza, her face flushed and giggling nervously was carefully avoiding any eye contact with the men. Normally high spirited and flirty Eliza's nervous demeanour alerted James suspicions further.

"Jimmy will need to watch his step," he observed. Eliza had clearly been keen to avoid any sort of banter and her studied avoidance of Jimmy was most unusual. Although emotionally detached from the situation James was mindful of the fact that Thomas was away facing significant risk at sea, and although he was friends with Jimmy it didn't sit easy with him if 'the two of them were carrying on behind the man's back.'

James decided that he would voice his concerns to Jimmy when the next opportunity arose. "I'll not pussyfoot around; it needs to be nipped in the bud before it goes too far, for all of their sakes. The trouble with Jimmy was that he always wanted it all, he's always held a torch for Eliza, if his suspicions were correct then all hell would let loose" James determined.

Suddenly hot and fidgety, the all too familiar agitation and stomach-churning caused him to break out into a sweat, and he found that he couldn't focus on the game. The din from the front room became overwhelming and hastily undoing his top collar he made his excuses.

"I'm going to sit this one out chaps I need some air."

"All right son" Arthur glanced up, "He's been a bit nervy lately," he explained.

"I suppose that whisky is stronger than we thought," mused Jimmy.

As James grabbed his jacket and shot through the front door, Eliza looking pretty as ever in her clover pink best dress with the sweetheart neckline manoeuvred her way around the table and back into the front room.

Patrick looked up, his glance following Eliza he whispered, "My, she looks as pretty as a picture; life on her dad's farm must be suiting her."

Jimmy kept his head down, studying his cards.

"Hey what goes on in there?" asked John, nodding towards the front room,

"It's suddenly very quiet."

"He be jee be lad." laughed Harold, "Women's games and natter that's all. Still, it keeps them happy I suppose."

John stood, stretched and glanced through the gap of the door which Eliza had left ajar.

Violet appeared to be dozing in an armchair in the corner of the room, her knees were covered in a grey blanket.

Frances sat opposite Norma and Joanie studying the contents of a teacup, whilst the other two ladies looked on with expectant expressions.

Lizzie sat gazing into her crystal ball, talking to Ruby quietly and every now and then sipping from a sherry glass.

Kathleen and Eliza and Lil were catching up on the latest gossip and news of Joanie's letters from Reg and Gordon's near-fatal crash landing, of Violet and Harold desperate hope for a letter from their sons, Eric and Clive.

Finally, the card game came to an end and a jubilant Arthur collected up his winnings which consisted of a pile of coppers and very little silver before he signalled that it was surely time to have 'a feed.'

Lil, Kathleen and Norma handed out tea plates to the men, Joanie put the kettle on the stove and Eliza and Lizzie collected the teacups from the front room, ready to wash up and start the refreshments.

"Tuck in everybody," Lizzie shouted cheerily over the chatter.

The men required no second invitation; they piled the wholesome wartime baking onto their plates.

"This is a good spread ladies," complemented John as he viewed the contents on the table.

Spam sandwiches, Lil's potato shortbread, Norma's bread pudding, a version of apricot flan made by Frances which consisted of carrots and plum jam, slices of rabbit pie, a large dish of peanuts which were a contribution from John himself and finally a few hard boiled eggs from Sam's farm. The company didn't hold with black market food generally, they were all aware that men risked their lives to bring food into the country but Sam didn't feel uneasy about half a dozen eggs on a rare occasion.

The ration booklets issued by the Ministry of Food allowed one egg per person a week although expectant mothers were allowed two. The booklets were precious and if they were lost a declaration had to be signed and there was one shilling fee payable. Even the Royal family were issued with ration books and they too had to register. Seasonal fruits and berries were not rationed because the Government couldn't guarantee a year-round supply, but jam-making still relied on the inventiveness of the women because sugar was in short supply. Bread and salt were not rationed either thankfully and bread pudding made good use of stale bread, even if it contained few dried fruits, it was filling and comforting.

"A good feed always soothes my nerves" sighed Norma. "I've developed a habit of reaching for something sweet when I'm feeling particularly hopeless, it works, a treat when I can get hold of a bit of sugar or jam that is. There will be a bit more of me for my Reginald to grab hold of when he gets home."

She smiled ruefully as she scratched around in her 'piny' pocket for her box of Swan Vesta matches and a stub of her last Player cigarette.

These were uncertain, troubling times and in these dark days they relied on each other for good company and cheer, either to receive comfort oneself or to offer encouragement and uplift, depending on the situation. Winston Churchill inspired them all with his wonderfully confident speeches but in the cold light of day, they were fully aware of Adolf Hitler's troop's swift advances over Europe. The stories that reached them filled the Mothers with dread and fear for their offspring. They were all very aware that it was only the Channel protecting Britain from her enemies and Norma's friend Nancy swore that she would, 'put her kids' heads in the gas oven before 'they' could get hold of them.'

Frances had no appetite, she crept quietly back into the front room and found Violet was still dozing so she tucked the blanket up further around the elderly ladies chest and over her cold arms. Just wanting to be on her own for a while, she sat quietly in the dimmed light, wondering about the days ahead. She pondered on Lizzie's prediction that Joseph was injured and was on his way home to her. She didn't dare quite believe, but her strange experiences and her recent dreams gave her hope.

She had tried to explain to Lizzie,

"Sometimes, when I wake the vast emptiness of my life engulfs me with such sadness. You know! It's like how it feels when you are the only one on the beach, surrounded by the flatness of the sea and a grey sky above, the loneliness is frightening. But walking on the same beach with Joseph holding my hand, then it becomes hauntingly beautiful. This is how my life would be, without him. This is how I feel, every morning when I wake, every evening when I climb the stairs for another long night."

Lizzie had listened and comforted with a hug and few words.

Frances gave herself a mental shake; she would take comfort in her friend's prediction. She trusted Lizzie wholeheartedly; after all she had never let her down before. Jumping up she called out,

"Enough of this, I'm becoming maudlin, play us a tune Ruby!"

Amongst the cheers and shouts of encouragement Ruby smilingly agreed. Taking the clarinet from the worn, black, leather case she stood herself in the middle of the kitchen.

"Right then, give a girl some space," she laughed and holding her clarinet high, facing John Parker with love shining in her warm brown eyes she played a rendition of ' Roses of Picardy,' and the company joined in, singing along.

James finished his third cigarette outside and hearing the tune came back into the 'warm lap of friendship' and joined in the singing.

Ruby followed with 'Bless em all' and finally the haunting melody of 'Glenn Miller's Moonlight Serenade.'

James and Jimmy whistled and John looked

on proudly. He thought that Ruby had never looked more stunning with her thick auburn curls swept to one side and her petite frame dressed in an emerald green satin blouse and a tight navy skirt showing off her curves. With a beautiful wide generous smile, she gazed up at him intently.

"Smiling just for me," he stared back at her with undisguised passion.

Feeling in his pocket for the small velvet box he decided and hoped that this was the right time, whilst they were surrounded by the love and laughter of Ruby's friends and Lizzie, whom Ruby thought of as a second mother.

"Hey folks, excuse me but may I interrupt for a moment?" John shouted loudly.

Everyone in the room stopped and looked on. John Parker was usually reserved and quietly spoken. Ruby stared at John in surprise, waiting.

The American officer took hold of Ruby's tiny hands, towering above her he smiled, nervously. Kissing her cheek he knelt down in front of her.

Fumbling in his pocket he took out the box and with shaking hands he opened it up and presented it to the blushing Ruby.

"Ruby, I've decided to ask you now, we all know that too many things can happen or get in the way in wartime, but I guess I'm still asking," he stuttered.

"Ruby darling, precious Ruby, will you marry me, will you be my wife?"

Ruby threw her arms around John, "Yes, oh yes," she cried.

He slipped the sparkling sapphire onto her finger amidst loud cheers of Well done! Smashing and a few other ribald comments that caused the ladies to tut!

The company rushed forward, shaking John's hand and kissing Ruby on her glowing cheeks. Arthur started to dance around; playing a tune on his spoons and Jimmy pulled his harmonica out of his jacket and began playing a popular George Formby song called 'When I'm Cleaning Windows.'

James joined in singing the cheeky lyrics and Eliza, unable to resist the music and fun caught hold of Frances's hands and they began jiving together, laughing and only stopping when they became breathless and tired of bumping into the furniture.

"Come on John, join in with us, you can't wriggle out of it" encouraged Jimmy.

Ruby grinned and walking over to John, she smiled up at him.

"Just for me?" she pleaded.

The effect of the spirits and the good company and Ruby's acceptance, caused a wave of homesickness to surge through John's being and he could feel the tears welling up. John realised that he had to 'get a hold of himself' pretty quickly or he would be faced with an embarrassing show of emotion, so hastily agreed to give them all a song.

"What the heck, I've just proposed to my lady in front of all of you good people so here goes!" and he sang tunefully a rendition of 'Don't sit under the apple tree for anybody else but me' whilst they all joined in with the popular song.

Jimmy played his harmonica and Kathleen hummed along as she glanced over at her daughter. Eliza 'hadn't opened up' yet and she hadn't pushed too much. Although she knew of her daughter's fun-loving nature she was still very surprised. It was no secret how much she adored Thomas.

"All in good time, I'll not bear down on her, to be honest, I just can't face it myself yet, let alone facing Tom or her dad with the news" she worried.

A call from the front room startled Kathleen from her deliberating about the best way to tackle the storm clouds gathering over her home. It was Harold, and he sounded distressed!

"Quick, it's our Violet, James, Lil, somebody, help her!"

James was sitting nearest the open front room door and so he rushed in with Lil close on his heels. He looked on in disbelief and with a sense of dread he knew, there was no mistaking. Recognising a human condition that he was now all too familiar with he caught hold of Harold's arm.

"It's too late, I think she's gone" he whispered quietly, looking gently into Harold's shocked face.

Lizzie rushed in and the rest of the company stayed respectfully back, only the ticking of the clock broke the stunned silence. Lil stifled a sob and the dazed husband stood, frozen.

Frances jumped up, calling out as she ran out of the back door,

"I'm off to fetch Doctor Price."

She hurtled down the darkened street to Doctor Price's home two streets away. The telephone lines were down so she knew that it was useless calling from the telephone box on the corner. Frances wasn't sure if her speed was because of Violet's need or perhaps because of the recent state of her nervousness, she had acted instinctively on seeing

Harold's stunned expression and hearing Lil's cry of distress.

Fortunately, the GP had been at home and he had responded immediately. Within one hour of his arrival Violet had been taken away in the ambulance accompanied by her trembling husband and a white-faced James, who had decided that he couldn't let his old friend and neighbour go alone.

Harold still clung to his wife's grey blanket, staring down at her cold, waxy white face, whilst the tears ran freely down his lined face. Wiping the tears with the cuff of his sleeve he spoke through broken sobs,

"I know to others she's just a grey-haired old woman, but not to me, for I still see the young girl that captured my heart with her beautiful warm smile and twinkling laughing, brown eyes. She was always full of mischief and laughter, and I was hers the minute I set my eyes on her, and amazingly she felt the same about me."

James was at a loss, he didn't know how to comfort the usually taciturn elderly man who was sitting next to him 'breaking his heart.' He decided that there weren't any words that would help at this point, and so he took a large white handkerchief out of his front pocket and handed it to Harold, who sobbed a thank you and roughly wiped his face.

"Do you know James, I always thought that I'd go first, I've outlived the doctor's expectations by a good few years. I mean we all have to pass over and leave some room for the young replacements," he explained in an attempt at putting the lad at ease, realising that he needed to 'catch a hold of himself now.'

James nodded.

The journey continued in silence as the ambulance travelled over the bomb-damaged roads on its way the hospital.

Back at Lizzie's the company of friends and neighbours sat together in the kitchen talking quietly. Norma suddenly cried out,

"I knew that she wasn't in good shape after losing her home, but little did I think that this would be our last little sing-song and the last time we'd have one of our 'get-togethers.'"

John Parker had wondered if he should tactfully leave but Ruby begged him to stay with her. Ruby sat at his feet, her tear stained face resting on his knee.

Lizzie soothed a sobbing Eliza.

"It was her time love. Everything and everyone has a beginning, middle and an end, it's the cycle of life."

Violet's sudden passing hadn't come as a total shock to Lizzie but she wasn't about to disclose 'her knowing,' it wouldn't do.

"Poor Eric and Clive," Frances whispered into the room. "Poor Harold."

Joanie, always capable and calm in most situations busied herself giving out strong cups of tea and tidying the food away.

"Who would have thought that when we got together this afternoon that we'd lose Violet." she pondered.

It was another hour before Sam would collect his wife and his daughter and nobody else made a move to leave. They all sat listening to the wireless playing low and to the ticking of the clock, finding a comfort in being together. Midnight had slunk in earlier hoping for a few titbits from the table and had now settled himself down at Jimmy's feet whilst Jimmy absent mindfully stroked his softness.

The minutes passed until they heard the footsteps outside becoming nearer and louder.

"Harold and James back already?" enquired Frances in surprise.

The door burst open, standing in the open doorway, large as life, handsome and smiling with open arms stood Thomas.

"Where's my sweetheart then?"

Eliza jumped to her feet and flung herself at Thomas, throwing her arms around his neck and wrapping her legs around his waist. He twirled her around laughingly and clutching her bottom he staggered and cried out,

"Gaud, you've filled out a bit love."

Kathleen thought that her heart would stop!

Frances cautiously glanced at Jimmy as Eliza buried her head in Thomas's collar and began to cry.

"Here we go." Thought Frances in dread as Thomas gave a puzzled look at Eliza.

Lizzie stepped forward,

"We've had a shock Thomas, Violet passed away in my front room not two hours ago, Harold's at the hospital. James went with him, what with their boys being away," she explained respectfully.

Thomas sat down heavily onto the nearest chair, still holding Eliza tightly and closely to him he tried to find the words to express his regret, but his mind had gone blank and no words came. What could he say? It was all too much right at this moment.

Joanie handed the dazed Thomas a small whiskey which he gratefully swallowed down in one gulp.

"Crikey, that not Lil's rhubarb wine" he spluttered in surprise.

Some of the tension dissipated following this remark and Ruby took the opportunity to proudly introduce her new fiancé

"This is Lieutenant John Parker, American Air Force" she smiled.

Thomas nodded and shook hands with John.

The company 'sprung back to life' and attempted to put Thomas at ease following the shock news. Lizzie explained that they had all decided to have a 'little get together' and had been enjoying a sing-song. They had left Violet to have a little doze.

"What with Harold and Violet being bombed out and all we thought that forty winks would do her the world of good."

Joanie told of Gordon's injuries and Jimmy talked of the factory being hit in the recent raids of the past week.

Eliza noticed Thomas's alarm and she hastily added that the boys were safe and that she and their sons were living with Sam and Kathleen back on the farm, laughingly adding

"Yes, and they are as naughty as ever."

Lizzie handed Thomas a dinner plate piled high with sandwiches and rabbit pie and Midnight took a chance and swiftly moved his allegiance from Jimmy to the owner of the food.

Frances laughed, "You don't miss a chance do you puss" as she bent forward to lift him up into her arms.

Suddenly Eliza jumped off Thomas's knee, knocking the plate of food into his lap.

"While we are making announcements Ruby, I've got one myself," she exclaimed nervously as she glanced over at Kathleen.

Kathleen stared in horror,

"Gaud our Eliza now's not the time" she gasped.

"It's not what you think it is mum" Eliza giggled, "It will be okay."

Kneeling in front of Thomas, Eliza leant towards him and gazed softly into his eyes.

"Thomas, I'm having your baby, you are going to be a dad again."

Jimmy was stunned, "Has she lost her marbles?" he silently questioned. He had wondered when she had fainted, thinking that maybe Eliza had 'slipped up' following 'a one-off' after the dance. It wasn't unknown in these times he had reasoned. But crikey, what's she up to now?

The room was silent following her announcement, Lizzie and Frances couldn't believe their ears and the others just waited for an angry reaction from Thomas, who after all had been away at sea for the past months.

Unbelievably Thomas gave a roar of laughter.

"Well! 'jumping ship' turned out to be more eventful in more ways than one love."

"What do you mean Thomas" Kathleen demanded.

"The ship was in the dock a couple of months ago for reloading, so I and another three chaps went ashore. We had a few too many, I fell asleep somewhere and they couldn't find me so, knowing that we'd all be in hot water if it was assumed that we'd all jumped ship, they had no other option than to return back on board without me. I cadged a lift and me and your daughter had a midnight rendezvous. I reported to the Pool Office two days later and explained. It didn't go down well as you can imagine. They made it very clear that this could be viewed as a serious offence and I could be jailed if they so decided. So, I took a special operations trip to make amendments, hence no letters. I've got five days leave now before I sign up again for another trip."

"Well, I never!" Kathleen sighed in relief.

"But you were so upset Eliza, why?"

"Oh, you know how I was last time mum and I was missing Tom" Eliza explained sheepishly.

Jimmy looked on and taking a deep breath called out,

"Time for another toast everybody, congratulations to you both."

Patrick stood and with a warm laugh he patted Thomas on his back in amazement.

"You crafty beggar," he joked and Eliza snuggled into Thomas, blushing.

Lil was secretly relieved that Jimmy might at last move on with his life now that he could see for himself how happy the couple were. Her nephew was a decent enough fellow she pondered, and she knew in her heart that he wouldn't have consciously wished Thomas any harm. But Eliza was very pretty and recently fate had seemingly thrown the two of them together. Many relationships were forged between those from totally different backgrounds and social standings during these times of war, some would work and some would fall apart at the first hurdle. Lil knew that standards of behaviour had changed somewhat since the war but she didn't want to see anyone hurt.

Jimmy resignedly accepted the way things had turned out and although his secret hopes were dashed; his hardy cheerful personality would carry him through.

"Perhaps when the war is over, if all's well and good then I just might make the move and travel as I've always wanted to." he dreamed. Australia and New Zealand had always held an attraction for him since he was a young lad. He had always enjoyed chatting to Thomas, hearing about the many places and strange customs and peoples that Thomas had met on his travels.

Jimmy's thoughts were suddenly interrupted by the loud throb of a motorbike engine which became louder and then suddenly cut out near the house.

"That sounds familiar" cried Thomas, and as he stood Sam entered the crowded kitchen, stopping abruptly when his eyes fell on his son-in-law.

"Well, it's good to see you lad, aye, the twins will be over the moon to see their dad" he cried, shaking Thomas's hand and patting him on the back enthusiastically.

Lizzie welcomed Sam and sat him down at the crowded table whilst Kathleen and Eliza rushed over to tell of the happy and sad news. Sam brushed his forehead, struggling to take in the awful shock of Violet's sudden departure from the world and the news that a new life would be coming into his own family.

John placed a small tot of Bourbon whiskey into Sam's cold hand and Sam gratefully 'knocked it back' in one go. A broad smile spread across his face as he realised that he'd just swallowed real whiskey. Ruby laughed and introduced John proudly, showing off her sparkling engagement ring.

Frances looked on at Ruby and John, so obviously in love, smiling and laughing, at Eliza and a very proud father to be who had his arms wrapped around his darling protectively, and who was now glancing over every now and then at Jimmy in a cautionary manner, sending a secret message of 'she's mine, don't touch.'

Thomas wasn't predisposed to bear a grudge and was usually inclined to be as good-natured as Jimmy, but Jimmy totally understood where Thomas's territorial behaviour was coming from.

Jimmy smothered a sigh, "Well Aunt Lil, Uncle Patrick, I think I'll make tracts then," and he hurriedly hugged Lizzie and pulled on his duffle coat ready to leave the company.

Patrick reacted quickly. "Come on Lil, time for us to be off too, thanks for a good evening everybody. I still can't believe what's happened to poor Violet; let me know what we can do for poor Harold will you Norma when they return from the hospital."

"I can't understand it myself yet either, it's as if my brain can't take it in, I can still see her sitting there in the chair." Lil explained, looking at no one in particular, gazing into the front room.

The company murmured in agreement and Patrick and Lil hurriedly followed Jimmy out.

Following their lead Sam took his chance to make a move, mumbling his excuses that he needed to get back because he had an early morning start. Besides, he felt awkward and it didn't 'sit easy with him' that they were all continuing on with their social occasion after poor Violet had only just 'popped her clogs.'

Making their farewells with lots of hugging and regrets about Violet's passing they were the next to leave. Thomas sat on the front of his motorbike, Sam pillion and Kathleen and Eliza squeezed into the sidecar. Lizzie quickly closed the door behind them, mindful not to shine any light out onto the street.

Joanie and Arthur next made their goodbyes and accompanied a worried Norma back home. The girls were staying with their aunt Gladys and this now left Norma alone in the house, waiting for Harold to return with James. Norma was glad of some support, not knowing what sort of condition Harold would be in on his return.

"He'd lost his home and his wife in one week, both of his sons were away fighting, 'Gaud' knows where," Norma whispered. Sighing she opened her back door and they all bustled in.

"I'll put the kettle on," she gushed, suddenly finding the quiet emptiness of her home distressing without her lively daughters.

"Leave it Norma," Joanie softly directed, "We are all awash with tea, sit down for a minute with us, we can just be still and wait for their return."

Norma planted herself down heavily in Reg's favourite armchair, next to Arthur and Joanie who had made themselves comfortable on the well-worn, comfy sofa. They all sat in silence and waited.

There was just the four of them left now from the get-together; Ruby and Frances helped Lizzie with the final clearing away whilst John was lost in thoughts of home.

John's parents had been immensely proud of their son when they heard that he had been made up to a 1st Lieutenant, and frankly very relieved when he had been grounded and 'safe.' They were distressed to hear of the loss of his aircraft and of some of his crew of course, but they didn't feel guilty, they were thankful that John had been spared.

No longer a pilot he had found it difficult to settle to routine but John had finally accepted his fate and put all of his leadership skills into his position as a ground crew officer. This was a 'full on' position which left him in charge of the many enlisted men on the base. He was responsible for overseeing the men and their duties, ensuring that all ran smoothly and that the base was managed safely and efficiently.

'When would he ever see his family again?' he wondered, in particular he was bothered that he hadn't written to his mother for a while and he resolved to put that right as soon as he returned to the base tonight. He appreciated the privileges that his status accorded him. The officer's accommodation enabled him to have some privacy, he needed some quiet now to sit down and write home in peace. Violet's sudden death had shaken him and he was ashamed of his laziness. Spurred on by an image of his mother receiving the news of his engagement he jumped up and called to Ruby.

"It's time to get back to the base honey." He hurriedly said his goodnights to the company, then he gave Ruby a crushing hug and left quickly. Ruby listened to the engine of the jeep as it roared into action outside and then faded away into the night leaving her with that awful sense of melancholy that twilight brought on.

Lizzie and Ruby invited Frances to stay for a while longer but Frances declined the offer, knowing that Lizzie was weary and besides more than a little upset about her good friend Violet's passing.

Hugging them both she wished them 'a goodnight and sweet dreams' and clutching a wriggling Midnight she made her retreat. Lizzie reached out to her at the last moment,

"Try not to be too despondent ducks, keep your chin up," she encouraged, her nut-brown eyes shining full of compassion for her lonely friend.

Frances smiled and softly closed the door.

CHAPTER 9.

"So, just you and me again puss," she whispered into his softness, "Let's hope that there won't be any more raids tonight."

Midnight meowed loudly as if in agreement. Frances climbed tiredly up the stairs to her bed, undressing quickly and dropping her blue silk dress in a heap on the lino she jumped into her cold bed, still wearing her underwear and stockings. Stretching out her arm she placed her earrings and locket on the bedside table, unpinned her heavy black locks of hair and promptly fell asleep.

Midnight sat on the end of her bed, watching, staring into the darkness, fully alert.

Frances slept fitfully, she dreamt of Joseph, she cried out in her troubled sleep, Midnight watched and waited!

Joseph crept into her room, trod softly on the creaking floorboards and climbed into her bed. Tenderly he pulled aside the tangled curtain of hair from her beautiful face and Midnight looked on. He could wait for his cuddles; it was enough at this moment just to luxuriate in his master's presence. Cautiously Midnight moved slowly up the bed and burrowed under the blankets to get warm and to be near the two humans who held his affections.

Joseph glanced at Midnight for a quick moment and laughed. "Hello puss, I've missed you too you old rascal."

The cat purred softly as Joseph tickled and petted him gently under his chin. He stretched out his well-fed sleekness and gave rough cat kisses in return.

Joseph did not want to wake his sleeping wife yet. He had waited for and imagined this moment for such a long time and now he wanted to savour every wonderful moment.

Frances's body was warm and soft and deliciously silky. He nuzzled into her slender neck, her perfume filled his senses and as he gently caressed her bare arms and her stockinged legs he wondered how he could have been so lucky to have such a beautiful woman for his wife.

How he had waited for this moment and had dreamt of this moment, to the point that sometimes he had been unclear whether he had dreamt or had in fact travelled in spirit to be with her.

Sorely tempted, Joseph suddenly lost all restraint and he buried his head into the softness of her breast and smothered his darling wife with passionate kisses.

Frances moaned softly and she turned into his arms. Opening her eyes, in her half-asleep state she again thought that she was dreaming, dreaming of Joe and herself, together in this sweet twilight world, and that he was making love to her.

Midnight meowed loudly and caught his paw in her tangled hair and Frances was suddenly alert and fully awake. Her emerald green eyes widened in recognition and her heart did a somersault in her breast.

"Oh my God, Joseph, it's you, it's really you," she cried and she started to sob, and then she laughed and she thanked God again and again as she clung onto him. Joseph laughed and shushed her as he 'rained down' hot kisses onto her face, and shoulders and her breasts.

Midnight blinked and jumped down and retreated underneath the bed. 'It was time to give his humans some privacy.'

Light flickered through the chinks in the blacked out window. The couple lay intertwined together in the light of early dawn and the coldness of the night still pervaded the bedroom. Neither noticed the coldness, they were oblivious to their surroundings as at this moment their spirits were lifted to a higher plane of reality.

Joseph and Frances had passed the night making urgent love to each other, and talking, questioning, reassuring, sleeping briefly and then clinging onto each other again, tenderly, desperately, never wanting these moments to come to an end.

Joseph poured out his story, half talking, half crying, as Frances held him in her arms, tightly. He haltingly explained how he had been injured in the fighting and how he had laid on the beach, feeling his life blood oozing out of him, feeling the pull of mortality slowly lessening.

The intense bombardment from the air and from the heavy German guns had destroyed most of the port facilities and under cover from the British Air Force the rescue boats and naval ships had done their best to lift the trapped army from the beaches to safety. In all of the confusion, and being very aware that they only had a limited time to evacuate before further Nazi troops arrived, it wasn't feasible to seek out the living from under the many dead bodies. The naval Command had to make difficult decisions, 'Any survivors would just have to take their chances or be taken prisoner by the Nazi's,' hopefully they would be treated well.

He whispered into her hair how he had lay cold in the wet, bloodied, sand, his leg was badly smashed, and how he had expected that any minute someone would come and 'finish him off.' So this was it, this is how my war will end, he'd accepted sadly, and the realization had brought a painful emptiness that had crept slowly through his being, and he's cried out for Frances. He had watched and waited for a seeming eternity in the awful silence, surrounded by the dead and dying bodies of his comrades.

When night fell it brought with it a freezing cold blackness and shivering he started to slowly and painfully drag himself over the bodies of his pals. Exhausted, he couldn't drag himself any further and so he had slumped onto a large rock and curled himself up behind it, in an effort to find some sort of shelter from the advancing tide that was creeping up towards him. Sleep evaded him as the agony in his right leg pierced his being with a hot burning fire of pain, he felt cautiously down his body, fearful of what he may find. The leg was still there, he continued feeling all the way down to his ankle, the bone protruded and he screamed. His hand was wet from the spray and dampness, and as he brought his hand up to his face he could smell and feel the stickiness of blood.

Joseph lay waiting for death, he knew that the

blood loss was heavy and he knew that if he did last until first light then there was every chance that the Jerries would find him or perhaps the sea would take him.

As he lay shivering his thoughts were of Frances back home, imagining her distress when she received the inevitable, dreaded telegram. He focused what was left of his energy into picturing her image, imagining that he was kissing her beautiful sensuous lips and telling her how much he adored her, and the last thing he saw in his mind's eye was her delicate face suddenly coming into focus, and her soulful, emerald green eyes staring back at him. Mercifully he then drifted into the oblivion of unconsciousness

Joseph had woken in a fog of cold and pain. Miraculously he had been discovered by a local, who's tan and white Springer Spaniel had ignored all desperate shouts from his owner to 'come back' and had wandered down amongst the carnage and shown interest in a body slumped under the boardwalk of the breakwater. The elderly owner managed to drag Joseph along with him, and despite them facing immense risk the villagers had hidden him and taken care of him.

Joseph had sustained heavy damage to his right leg, an injury to his forehead above his right eye and damage to his right ear which had resulted in some hearing loss, other than that he had survived. Joseph had been kept heavily drugged with alcohol and whatever medication that could be found, to alleviate and to smother his cries of pain as his leg was crudely set back into place. Initially, he had existed in a state of sporadic delirium, drifting in and out of reality, not knowing where he was or who he was with.

Joseph told of the following weeks, of existing on a cycle of pain and how at times he had cried for The Almighty to put an end to his suffering. Eventually, the infection in his leg cleared, the broken bones had started to heal, the bloodied flesh and bandages no longer caused offence, and his memory cleared.

Many months passed before Joseph was in a condition where it was safe to move him. Finally, the French resistance had made themselves known to him, he had been recruited to help, and he had spent the last year working with them. Joseph had immense admiration for their courage and was thankful for his life and he had grown very fond of the family that had taken him in, particularly for the wilfully, disobedient Pepe, who had saved his life that morning. Joseph knew that he was amazingly lucky not to have been made a prisoner of war, or worse and that he had evaded capture purely because of the keenness of a hungry dog that had been hopeful of finding some sort of sea bounty to fill his empty stomach that morning.

When an opportunity finally arrived, on a very dark night with little moon, he was brought across the narrow stretch of water that was the English Channel in a small fishing boat, with two other rescued British soldiers. They were dropped off at a lonely coastal spot and they had hugged and thanked the brave men that had risked life and limb to bring them home.

The local hospital had treated the men, but as for Joseph's leg? The doctor had pronounced that

"It's as good as it can get dear boy I'm afraid, but they did well to save your leg," he'd added as an afterthought.

His unit had been notified and finally Joseph had been discharged because of his loss of hearing and lameness. A letter had been despatched to Frances which she hadn't yet received, but Joseph had chosen not to write, he wanted to see her face when he walked in the door, finally home.

So, he had returned, limping, and always would be, because his leg had been set badly, but still, home, and in one piece! Finally, he was free, to be together with his love. They will share their passions and their jealousies and their laughter, and with a bit of good luck live out the war and the rest of their lives together.

"I don't know what's ahead of us Fran," Joseph whispered, "but whatever happens we will face it together, and perhaps one day we will return to France, and I will take you to meet the wonderfully brave people that saved my life at risk of their own, for if it wasn't for their courage I wouldn't be here now."

"But I knew you were coming home Joseph, she saw you, Lizzie, walking home to me in her crystal ball, and me and Lizzie, we saw it in the tea leaves," Frances related eagerly.

Joseph laughed, "Oh! You women and your fancies are a delight, how I've missed you all, even your queer ideas, but what does it matter?"

Then he turned to his darling wife and whispered into her hair,

"What does anything else matter, you are all

that matters now Fran, despite all the fighting and killing, I do believe that for all man's stupidity the light within us all survives, and shines even in the most horrific circumstances. I've seen it! Love is all that matters, love is all you see." And he kissed her again and again!

***

About the Author

Betty Rose was born in Coventry and is the youngest of six children. She grew up in the 50s and 60s when Coventry's engineering and car manufacturing was booming.

She worked as a Registered Mental Health Nurse until her retirement, 2 years ago.

She still lives in Coventry with her husband and Milly dog.

"I was born in 1951 and I grew up in a hardworking, earthy neighbourhood amongst many who had lived through WW2 and who shared their experiences with sadness and humour."

"I'm a Coventry kid, always will be."

Printed in Great Britain
by Amazon